WHEN PAST AND FUTURE MEET . . .

Driving along the road, Carmelita suddenly veered. It was too late; the strange men in primitive costume were before her, upon her—one stricken in the road, dead . . .

In the cage before him, Fusaka saw what he never thought he would see—an enormous black furry monster with great raking claws and a blunt feral muzzle that grunted and hissed and snapped at its confining bars—a species that had long ago disappeared from Earth . . .

Van der Reis was lying on the couch when he screamed. Even as the woman watched, his tunic faded, his eyes lost their luster, his face became a mere sketch. He simply . . . ceased to be!

Artery of Fire

by Thomas N. Scortia

POPULAR LIBRARY • NEW YORK

All POPULAR LIBRARY books are carefully selected by the POPULAR LIBRARY Editorial Board and represent titles by the world's greatest authors.

POPULAR LIBRARY EDITION

Library of Congress Catalog Card Number: 72-79422

Published by arrangement with Doubleday & Company, Inc.

A much shorter version of the present novel under the same title appeared in *The Original Science Fiction Stories*, March 1960.

PRINTED IN THE UNITED STATES OF AMERICA

For Ron Joakim Julin
Of longboats past and clippers present.

I met a traveler from an antique land
Who said: Two vast and trunkless legs of stone
Stand in the desert. . . . Near them on the sand
Half-sunk, a shattered visage lies, whose frown,
And wrinkled lip, and sneer of cold command,
Tell that its sculptor well those passions read
Which yet survive, stamped on these lifeless things,
The hand that mocked them, and the heart that fed:
And on the pedestal these words appear:
"My name is Ozymandias, king of kings:
Look on my works, ye Mighty, and despair!"
Nothing beside remains. Round the decay
Of that colossal wreck, boundless and bare
The lone and level sands stretch far away.

"Ozymandias"—Percy B. Shelley (1792-1822)

Chapter One

A.D. 2020
H MINUS FOUR HOURS

The Artery is dead now. No, not dead. Rather suspended in life, for in thirty hours it will flame forth again, linking the outer and inner planets in a pulsing umbilical cord of blue ionization. For the moment the transjovian space is dead except for the innumerable pinpoints that mark the asteriod debris. (It was once thought that these might be the fragments of a planet in the space between Mars and Jupiter, shattered by some ancient cosmic disaster. The first exploration of the outer planets disproved this theory. The asteroids are clearly the remnants of the planetary mantle of Pluto, lost at the moment the Solar System captured the dark planet from its near cometary orbit.)

The great ore plains of Pluto are far from still. Silent vaguely manlike shapes move heavily across them, finishing the realignment of the great ionization tubes. The orbiting Plutonian lens station drifts silently, the last lens station already in its new orbit after being carefully towed across the ecliptic plane. Sunward, the Black Field Lens Stations revolve silently in their cislunar orbit while the Nodal Lens Group hangs in metastable orbit above the revolving satellite, its ever-decaying orbit adjusted by silent jets of cesium ions.

In the immediate area of the Black Field Stations, a

faint radiance flickers, grows stronger, subsides, grows again, pulsing with a periodicity of slightly over five seconds. It is a cold white radiance, only faintly visible. Only one group of observers detects it at this point.

The transit ship *Orion*, leaving parking orbit for its months-long journey to the Martian terraform colony, passes very close to the near-point source of the radiation. On board André LeBlanc, a nuclear engine technologist, stands beside the pilot, looking out through the foreport. He starts. My God, he says, that's impossible.

What's impossible, the pilot demands, and LeBlanc says the radiance looks like Cherenkov radiation. This means nothing to the pilot until LeBlanc explains that Cherenkov radiation is a common phenomenon around nuclear reactions. It is visible light generated when a particle traveling through glass or other medium exceeds the local speed of light.

That's ridiculous, the pilot insists, since light speed is the limiting speed of the universe. Light speed in a vacuum, LeBlanc corrects him.

What the hell do you think that is out there? the pilot demands, pointing into cislunar space.

LeBlanc knows that Cherenkov radiation is impossible in space. Its existence would imply a particle exceeding the speed of light in a vacuum, an impossibility. Of course, LeBlanc is only a technician and hardly equipped to speculate on such an apparent paradox.

He knows only that nothing can travel in a vacuum faster than light. Therefore, it cannot be Cherenkov radiation.

He is, of course, terribly wrong.

Running north from Manila is the famous Dagupan zigzag road, its ancient surface now widened and flattened to accommodate the surface-sensitive ground effects machines that move along its sinuous course. There is another more direct route, the Naguilan Road, that skirts the mountainous intricacies of the zigzag, but for the leisurely traveler the scenic beauty of the northern Luzon mountains, with their lush tropical growth, is reward enough for the special alertness required to navigate the road.

For Carmelita Guadalupe Concepcion O'Fallon, the last day of her leave carried a special excitement, since she was journeying north to visit her brother Rodriguez, who was a supervisor on one of the great coastal chlorella plantations. She had already passed through several similar plantations on the plains south of Manila, threading her way through the towering plastic columns of bubbling nutrient and green algae, waving at the men harvesting the oil-rich chlorella at the base of one of the towers. Every inch of plains was crowded with the great columns, drinking up the energy of the clouded tropical sun that fed the fecund growth of the mutant algae. The towers in this area produced an oil-rich algae which, when processed produced a fine lubricant. Secondary fractions were hydrogenated in plants near Manila to produce a good grade of cooking oil. The plants were productive at least six months of the year in spite of the omnipresent condensation clouds that drifted over the islands from the heat-sink below Mindanao, where the billion-kilowatt nuclear plant discharged its cooling waters into the sterile bay.

Carmelita had hoped to spend two days with her brother, but her group leader, Mario Muletti, had contacted her in Manila just before she left. She now knew that she would be able to spend only the evening with her brother before returning to the Computer Station in Pelambang for her duty with the Artery. She had hoped that she would not come on duty until transmission had been re-established, but her counterpart, Emir, had taken ill at the last minute. It was a small annoyance, and she quickly shed her low spirits as the trip progressed. Once she stopped at the edge of the smooth road and climbed from the idling machine to shinny up a Jabo tree and pluck one of the soccer ball-size fruits. Although she had been on Luzon now for over a week, she rarely saw the heavy pulpy orange-like Jabo of the mountains. They were rare enough with the encroachments of modern civilization; the once-dense growths of the island had been reduced to a few isolated patches in the mountains where it was still commercially impractical to establish processing stations or chlorella plantations.

She had set the machine on automatic and was busily stripping the three-quarter-inch-thick rind from the Jabo when it happened. The light was already dimming and she knew that she would not reach Dagupan until well after nightfall, but the last twenty miles of the road were well lighted. Moreover Dagupan, with its well-planned city street grid, was easy enough to get about in, despite its having grown in recent years to well over a million in population.

Because of the early dusk in the mountains she did not notice any movement on the edge of the road. Indeed, as she recalled later, there may not have been any. The small group of men seemed to appear as if by magic in the middle of the road. At one instant the flat compacted roadbed was empty, and then before her, too late to brake, there was the group of ten scantily dressed men, leading a waddling yellow dog. The men appeared confused and milled about on the road. Several saw her and started to run to the edge of the road. In the next instant the machine had plowed into the group and was sliding off the side of the road. The air cushion encountered the sudden irregularity of the road gutter and beyond that the ragged turf and jutting rock of the virgin ground. In a second the machine had flipped on its side and Carmelita was flying through the air, clutching the half denuded Jabo as if somehow it might preserve her life.

For a long moment, she lay stunned, the breath driven from her body. Her sight flickered with a thousand imaginary lights, and she felt a heavy pain at the base of her skull. When sensation gradually returned, she discovered that her hands were bound firmly behind her, lashed to a heavy stick. A dirty face with scraggly teeth grimaced a bare six inches from her face when she opened her eyes. She gasped involuntarily. Thick lips said something in a language she did not understand. She winced at the spray of saliva as the savage spoke.

Rough hands grabbed her arms and forced her to her feet. She felt bony wiry hands tug at the bonds on her wrists, half supporting her weight. She pulled free and turned. A second figure loomed behind her. In the half light of dusk she saw that, except for a rope about his waist from which a breechcloth was suspended, he was completely nude; his bare feet were splaytoed and dusty. He was carrying a bow of some dark wood, and several arrows protruded from a crude quiver on his back. The bow was not the European sort with a double curve and distinct hand grip. It appeared to be a single sweeping piece of mahogany, the inside hollowed by scraping; the ends were drawn together with a fiber cord. The arrows themselves were of reed, feathered with chicken feathers. The arrow he carried in the same hand with the bow was tipped with a hammered iron point perhaps six inches long with rows of opposed barbs. It was a particularly vicious tip, she realized, since once in the flesh it could neither be withdrawn nor pushed through. At his waist, thrust through the fiber cord that held the breechcloth was a curved knife of dull bronze or brass, shaped much like a linoleum knife with a thin polished edge.

The two men grabbed her arm and propelled her forward across the road. On the other side the rest of the band squatted before a campfire they had built while she was unconscious. There were nine of them in all. A tenth, she corrected herself, as a deep groan came from the edge of the group. She saw a sprawled shape at the edge of the firelight and realized that she must have injured one of them in the last instant when she was frantically braking the car.

The man behind her forced her to her knees before the fire. She leaned back trying to get some slack in her bonds. They were already cutting painfully into her flesh. She eyed the men around the fire. They were all relatively small, none of them over five-seven, she thought. They were dark and appeared Micronesian, with straight black hair and relatively long noses. All of them were dressed in the same primitive fashion and all carried the simple mahogany bows she had seen earlier in the hand of her first captor. They eyed her silently. Finally one turned to the sprawled figure, crouched over it, and said something in the same unknown tongue.

What were they, she wondered, and where had they come from? They looked very much like the pictures of early Igorots she had seen but the tribes, particularly around Baguio, had been farmers for a century now and had abandoned most of their earlier customs. She eyed the curved brass knife, remembering one of the customs of the Ibaloi and Kankanay tribes, and shuddered. Her throat felt suddenly very tight.

An older man appeared from out of the shadows, tugging on a fiber leash. At the end of the leash a small yellow dog, fat and gravid with heavy brown nipples swollen with milk, dug its paws into the earth. The older man gave a disinterested tug and the dog fell forward. The man dragged it into the circle by the campfire. A second later two other men carried the wounded man forward into the light. This too was an older man, although she had difficulty in ascertaining just how old. As with most savages, age came quickly to these people, and the wounded man could easily have been anywhere between thirty and sixty. His side, she saw, was smeared with blood that oozed from an open wound. One arm flopped at an odd angle. She wondered with the rough handling that he was receiving that the fracture had not yet compounded itself.

The man with the dog turned. With one hand he grabbed the bitch and rolled her on her back. Carmelita gasped as the firelight flashed on the upraised brass knife. In an instant blood gushed from the dog's throat, and while two others pinioned the thrashing animal, the man with the knife laid open the abdomen. The amniotic sac, heavy with the five fetuses, popped from the abdomen like an inflated balloon. The knife flashed again, and amniotic fluid gushed out over the still quivering animal. A gnarled hand ripped one of the half-formed young from the sac, and the flashing knife stripped flesh from the pink fetus.

She watched in horror as the first man turned and offered the flesh to the wounded man. His eyes opened, widened in pain, and he received the quivering flesh. Slowly he masticated it and then fell back exhausted. Carmelita felt her stomach churning at the sight. She knew from school that the Igorots had practiced cynotherapy, but the difference between the aseptic Latin word and the bloody reality of the moment was sickening. She strained against her bonds.

The savage holding the corpse of the bitch spoke in a low guttural voice, and the one who had slaughtered the bitch turned, his eyes wide. He smiled evilly, exposing yellowed snag teeth. As she watched in horror, he came slowly toward her, the bloody brass knife outstretched. Oh, God, she thought, this is insane. No, no. His intent was obvious. He grasped her hair and pulled her head to the side, eying her profile. She tried to struggle but other hands pinioned her.

She screamed once and a rough hand slapped her across the mouth, bringing the salty taste of blood to her tongue. The man with the knife grunted and brushed away the hand that had struck her. Of course, she thought insanely, the head must be perfect . . . without bruise or wound. She watched with mute horror as the knife wielder knelt and almost gently placed the curved brass blade against her throat. She closed her eyes and waited, sensing the bite of the point on her flesh, knowing that in another instant it would rip through her throat and spill her blood on the ground. Someone would find her headless corpse eventually, she thought hysterically. What would he think? Where would these impossible savages have gone by then?

She tensed, waiting. Then, as though the cords about her wrists seemed to evaporate, she felt the restraining stick fall and her arms came free. She opened her eyes. A twig in the campfire snapped. There was no other sound. Nor was there any sign of the Igorots who had a moment before held her captive.

Only the fire blazing. She massaged her wrists to restore circulation. Finally, her heart still beating with fear, she climbed the embankment to the roadway. She was close to weeping at the sudden reprieve, but she knew she must make no noise. What if they were still around?

She stood swaying, feeling the weakness invade her limbs. In the last minute before she sank to the ground in a half faint, she saw the lights of an approaching machine rounding the far curve. She was dimly aware as the machine stopped. She dimly saw two men approaching. Then they were lifting her, asking if she were all right. She began to weep hysterically, quite uncontrollably.

"It's very strange," Terrence McDow said, gesturing at the port. The glass curved gently before them, following the curvature of the spherical Black Field Master Station. Outside the moon loomed large and scabrous in the upper right quadrant. The darkside of Earth twinkled below as the omnipresent clouds scudded across the patches of light that marked the great megalopolises of the Eastern Hemisphere. In spite of the phenomenal growth of the Asian cities, the major cities of the world were still in the West. Later that night they would paint great splotches of color across the globe below. Not even the omnipresent clouds could completely mask the outpouring of radiance from a hundred million souls clustered in one relatively small area.

"We're accustomed to it when we're receiving beam transmissions," McDow said, "but this is the first time we've seen the radiation when only the Black Field itself is operating."

"That's not quite true," Norman Bayerd said, leaning his wasted body forward in the prosthetic chair. "We saw several instances of it a year ago during periods when the pulses were interrupted."

"Cherenkov radiation," McDow said. "It has to be that. There's no other explanation."

"Which means a tachyon flux," Bayerd said. "That's the only thing that can produce Cherenkov radiation in space."

Which was something André LeBlanc, the technician aboard the *Orion*, had not known. In spite of the virtual dependence of every human being on the Artery, the complexity of the effects associated with the plasmoid beam transmission and the radiation phenomena associated with the Black Field were not widely known. Schoolboys might be aware that tachyon fluxes existed, but the peculiar character of the fluxes within the Black Field did not reach the schoolbooks. A technician such as LeBlanc would discount Cherenkov radiation in space. After all, even in 2020 most technicians were not really aware that there were particles that could travel faster than light, that indeed could not travel slower than the speed of light in a vacuum.

"When's that damned research team returning to the station?" Bayerd demanded.

"They won't be back for another week," McDow said, rubbing his dark shining pate. He had lost about 50 percent of his hair at the age of thirty-five, but he preferred to shave the rest. His scalp was uneven, showing surprising lumps and ridges that spoke of peculiar sutures in the skull beneath. "You know, they want Earthside to run a series of model studies after the last transmission. I suppose, if they can devise a proper computer model, we'll be getting all sorts of wild-eyed theories on how the Black Field partitions the kinetic energy of the beam and why the partition effect has to produce a tachyon flux."

"Van der Reis has had them in his hair for the past three days," Bayerd said. "I finally ordered him to chase them out of the Pelambang Station until transmission resumes. We can't have our computer facilities cluttered with a lot of theoretical studies at this critical time. The political situation below is getting much too tense for any further interruption of fuel transmission from Pluto."

McDow rolled his eyes upward and pushed away from the port. He half walked, half floated across the space. The centrifugal force at this point on the exterior of the spherical station was attenuated. They were too close to the axis of rotation, barely a quarter of the station radius. "The idiots," he said softly. "You certainly don't think they'd start making war noises again?"

"There's a special kind of insanity about our

species," Bayerd said tiredly. He was feeling more fatigued than usual. Even the light gravity of the station still weighed his atrophied muscles. The weakness had become increasingly pronounced to him in spite of the relative weightlessness in which he moved. Had he still been on Earth, the physical decay with advancing Cushing's Syndrome would have doomed him to a fading life of complete invalidism. "No," Bayerd said, "they won't fight, but they will maneuver in every fashion possible to increase their share of fissionables."

"When are you going Earthside?" McDow asked.

"I thought I'd make my last inspection in half an hour," Bayerd said. "In the meantime, I'll look in on the transmission crew on Pluto."

"I wish you wouldn't," McDow said. His dark face smiled apologetically, "You make them nervous. They're very tense already."

"Christ, we're all tense," Bayerd said. "I know you think I'm a mother hen, but the Artery is my whole life. I can't stand sitting in this damned chair, isolated from the rest of the world, and let them tinker with my baby."

McDow came over to him and placed a heavy arm on the back of his prosthetic chair. The arm was heavily freckled where it protruded from the short sleeves and was covered with a thick growth of coarse reddish-brown hair. He said, "Everything will be all right. It'll go smoothly."

"I'm worried," Bayerd admitted. "There's been friction in the crew, particularly since the telecast on the census irregularities. Do you think they really tried to falsify it?"

"The census?" McDow shrugged. "I doubt if there's been a dishonest census since the Artery was built. Not when a region's share of the limited fissionables we bring back depends on a *per capita* rationing system. Everyone is very busy policing his neighbor. You know the kind of regional jealousy we'd had to deal with."

"I suppose so," Bayerd said tiredly. "I'm afraid the tension is getting to me as well. Still, I think I'll shrenk out to the accelerator."

"As you wish," McDow said. "Only be careful. Don't provoke anyone needlessly."

"I'm not an old woman," Bayerd said.

"No, but you demand a great deal more than most humans are capable of giving."

"Perhaps," Bayerd said and keyed the chair. Gyros rotated it slowly, and faint pulses of compressed air sent it drifting out of the room and down the corridors. He was drifting toward the axis of rotation where the Shrenk units were arrayed. While the complex pantographs that controlled the distant Shrenk robot bodies would be operated in a gravity field with no inconvenience, they were somewhat easier to handle in a zero-gravity environment. For this reason and because of Bayerd's physical disability, they had decided to locate them at the north pole of the station. At the time the station was built, of course, he was still relatively active, but it was obvious even then that his strength was declining. He himself had elected finally to remain permanently on the station. After all he told himself, what had Earth left to offer him. Family? Career? The Artery was his family, his career, and on Earth he would have become a helpless invalid, ending his days in a vegetable existence. Here at least he had mobility and a sense of belonging to something important, of living a useful life.

In the zero-gravity area, he was able to leave his chair and move more freely about. He floated from the prosthetic chair and drifted across the Shrenk chamber to one of the cubicles. He floated his limbs into place in the harness, fitting his fingers into the feedback gloves, his legs into the leg braces, resting his haunches lightly on the seat. Before him the Shrenk mask floated like an inverted bowl, the lens glistening dully in the red light of the cubicle. When he placed his head in the mask, his eyes would look into mirrored screens and he would see and with his limbs sense all the impulses reaching the Shrenk robot, wherever it might be. Connected with that distant metal body by c-cube radio, he was for practical purposes an intelligence embodied in the robot.

He leaned forward and activated the harness. Then he positioned his face in the mask and adjusted himself to the pressures of the arms, legs, and torso as that distant second self signaled the feedback somesthetic units of the harness, telling him that he was standing, arms outstretched, legs akimbo, that he was. . . .

Norman Bayerd. . . .

Suddenly in an instant as the speed of light cubed half the diameter of the Solar System away poised in a massive, looking out over. . . .

"You're a liar!"

The pent violence of the voice hissed in his ears, jarring him from his reverie. He stood on the edge of the precipice, feeling a sudden vertigo, a sense of disorientation, so that the star-flecked sky of Pluto into which he was staring seemed to writhe and pulse like the black surface of something alive.

Then he was over it and filled with a quick anger. Just for an instant he had felt somehow divorced from the reality that stretched out before him. You could lose yourself in the blackness of that sky, he told himself.

Standing on the very brink of creation . . . looking out through the infinite distances and knowing that there was nothing between you and the nearest point of light but endless emptiness. Nothing, not even the tiniest speck of rock, nothing but the sheer impassable loneliness of interestellar space.

"I'll break your swinish head," a second voice said.

Bayerd moved to the edge of the precipice, his heavy forelegs raising puffs of volcanic dust, which arced in low parabolic sheets back to the corduroyed rock, which still showed the flow patterns of ancient lava. He looked out over the vast polar tableland that stretched from this one prominence to the horizon, searching for the two figures near the southern tip of the great smelters. He adjusted his vision to infrared to take advantage of the heat radiating from the smelters and the ionization chambers and stepped up the magnification. The two men were near the far end of one of the massive conveyor belts that brought the pulverized uranium hydride from the great beds to the south. The image of four-legged massive bodies danced before his eyes. The images shimmered in the schlieren distortion of hot hydrogen spewing from the decomposing ore in the smelters.

"No Bosch speaks to me so," the first voice said. One of them raised a malletlike fist.

"Amazonian grave robber," the second voice sneered, and both figures moved in for contact.

"Stop it," Bayerd yelled. For an instant both robots froze motionless amid the glowing towers and throbbing chambers of the plain.

"Trubner, Sanchez," Bayerd demanded. "What's got into you two?"

"This smelling pig has a tongue that wags at both ends," Trubner said.

"Stop it! Any more of that and I'll put you on report," Bayerd threatened.

"Whose tongue wags too much now?"

"You too, Sanchez. We're cutting our deadline too close without any private wars."

"Sanchez is to blame," Trubner said thickly. "He and his lies about the Liechtenstein robbery and . . ."

"You heathen Germans would steal food from your mother's grave," Sanchez cut in hotly.

"I said that's enough," Bayerd snapped. "We've no time to fight among ourselves. Every minute the Artery is out of action means the power shortage Earthside becomes more critical. The Liechtenstein census trouble is just a taste of what's to come."

He paused for a moment, thinking of home and the darkened cities and the building tension. It was only a matter of time until the situation blew up in their faces unless . . .

He cut to the command net and said, "All right, can all of you hear me? Check in." Trubner and Sanchez acknowledged immediately, with Chang, Girard, and Muletti coming in seconds later.

"Gentlemen," Bayerd said, "we're two-thirds through our count-off. That gives us barely four hours to beam time. The power shortage back home is now a Class 'A' emergency. That means power rationing to private homes and to all but critical functions. We've run into delays here that we didn't anticipate."

He paused, listening to the murmur of agreement.

"We can't afford the luxury of quarreling among ourselves," Bayerd said. "Chang, you're senior group leader here. I want a report on the next man who starts trouble. You and your crews are all under military jurisdiction here, and I'll use every bit of that authority up to and including court-martial proceedings if there's any more of this bickering."

He cut from the circuit and snorted in disgust. Complete gibbering idiots, he thought. He switched to the "A" net and said, "Terry, did you get all of that?"

"They're all tense with the power shortage and the political situation Earthside," McDow said quietly. He sighed, and for a moment Bayerd had the odd illusion that the man was still standing beside him. Instead he was nearly three and a half billion miles away on the Black Field Station orbiting nearly a million kilometers from Terra. But, Bayerd thought wryly, even that wasn't true. Actually he was perhaps fifty feet away if he were still on the station's metering deck, less if he were on the Commo Bridge. The paradox made for some confusion in thinking unless . . .

"I've got some news that should take your mind off your trouble," McDow said drily.

"That sounds ominous," Bayerd said. He adjusted his sight to watch Girard and Muletti far inside the accelerator area as they stripped a foot-thick shield from one of the towering resonators of the accelerator. The chambers of the accelerator itself stretched far beyond his vision, like a fantastic metal Midgard serpent encircling Pluto's arctic circle.

"Our guests are coming a day early," McDow said. "The message was waiting when I got to the Commo Bridge."

"Mendoza and Gilchrist? Mendoza promised me

he'd keep that rabble-rouser out of our hair until after beam time."

"Apparently the good councilman from Greenland has found some new ammunition. He's bringing a friend of yours."

"Who?"

"Adrianne Patel," McDow said.

For a silent moment Bayerd considered the implications of the statement. He'd rather have ten Gilchrists on hand rather than her. He'd counted on Mendoza's presence to act as a counterbalance to Gilchrist, but her presence more than tipped the balance. The political atmosphere could well become tense.

"How long do I have?"

"Barely an hour."

"What are they trying to do?" he demanded angrily. "Catch us with our house dirty?"

"It would appear so. We wouldn't have this much warning if Mendoza's secretary hadn't radioed us from the Antilles Shuttle Field just after they took off."

"The shuttle?" Bayerd asked. "I thought they were going to shrenk up."

"No, Mendoza's man said Gilchrist wanted to make a personal inspection. It *is* strange," McDow added slowly.

"I don't have time," Bayerd said. "All of our crews are understaffed for the changeover, and I still have to check in with the Pelambang Computer Station."

He thought for a moment and then he said, "I want a news blackout on what's happening Earthside until I tell you otherwise. We can't have any more trouble with the crew." As if that would solve the major problem, Bayerd thought. After five years of jockeying for a bigger slice of the very finite power pie, national tempers at home were at the breaking point. The problem among the engineering crew was only a pallid reflection. Like the accusations last week that the census reports of the Liechtenstein District had been falsified. If only they could have delayed the Artery changeover a year. . . . No, the situation would only have worsened with the delay.

"I've got another hour's work just checking the calibration on the remote metering circuits after I get back from Pelambang," he told McDow. "Can you keep the firemen amused until I get back?"

"There's the planetarium," McDow suggested.

"Good. Take care of it, will you?" Bayerd said and cut from the circuit.

For seconds he stood, feeling the tensions of his body. Patel! This was the end. As if there wasn't enough pressure on him. It would be so good, he thought, just to lie down and rest. He should never have allowed them to persuade him to handle the changeover. He should instead have allowed someone younger, more resilient to step into this position. They would have allowed him token supervision, any pretense that would allow him to continue his circumscribed life away from the debilitating gravity field of Earth.

He realized that he would have insisted, however, even if they had not wanted him to do the job. That someone else, some other hand, should touch this creation of his was unthinkable. He had worked and fought for the Artery until it was the very core of his life. Everything in life that had meaning for other men (lesser men, he told himself) he had turned his back on . . . love, the easy decline of advancing years (yes, even honor, if the truth be known . . . if the word had any meaning in this day . . .), all of this he had set aside in this supreme effort of his life.

Even her. . . . He thought of Adrianne, her dark eyes large and serious and filled with the mist of a dozen lost years. He had loved her once, he supposed, but that was the price one paid for loving a strong woman. Much too strong to stand aside and silently assent to the driving ambitions of even her chosen man. The days were past when women of her race nodded silently in assent and bowed their heads to the need and the demands of their men. She had disagreed with him and seen this master achievement of his as something dangerous and finally disastrous. So she had fought him and fought him still.

And came now again to the field to fight him again. Well, he promised himself, he'd play the part of the wounded old lion. Let her come with all of the others. They might pull him down, but a good many of them would go with him.

For an instant he felt lost and completely divorced from all that humanity meant. A deep sorrow welled up in him from some hidden depth. He knew that at this crucial moment, he should not leave, that his job was here and now. The impulse was overpowering; no one would certainly miss him just for those few moments. He thought of that other distant body, wondering if the automatic control still functioned as smoothly. It had been almost two weeks since this overwhelming sense of *weltschmerz* had seized him and he had not needed the solace of that distant surrogate existence. Now he found he wanted it very badly.

He left the body on Pluto with a flick of the hidden switch on his Shrenk panel and was elsewhere.

It was a secret elsewhere, one he had carefully hidden from the casual eye since years before when he had altered the records of his Earthside activities and diverted this one device to serve as the only bastion of sanity he could find.

He found he was walking up a long flight of stairs. The transition from the automatic control in Pelambang, which only he knew about, to his real control of the body was smooth and effortless. He could almost feel the young synthetic muscles within the moving legs, the pulse of biceps and triceps, all unreal, of course.

It was morning he realized, a bright, relatively smogfree morning, certainly not more than 8:00 A.M., from the position of the sun. He entered the airlock doors and crossed the small lobby of the building. It was still deserted. Apparently the night watchman was off duty and the day man had not yet appeared. He shrugged, thinking that he should complain to the management about it. God knows, the streets of New York were terrible enough at night, but even during the day a lapse of the security watch might well be the invitation to trouble. Then he smiled to himself, thinking that all this really meant little to him who was more vulnerable and, in this body, more dangerous than any of the roving brigands of the decaying city.

The levitator bore him swiftly to the twentieth floor, and he whistled at the third door in the corridor. The machine within the walls compared the sonic print of his whistle with its identity bank, and the door slid open. The apartment was small, barely two and a half rooms, with concealed cooking facilities and a bed that rose from the floor in the living area. The bed was in the center of the room now, rumpled-looking and occupied.

She always delighted him with her fresh olive face peeking out from under stark white sheets. He preferred white because of her complexion. A part of his mind suggested to him that his alter ego had chosen her because of her resemblance to someone else, but he put that out of his mind very quickly.

The mass of sheets quivered and then exploded in flying fabric. "Oh," she cried out in the silence, "I knew it had to be you when I heard the whistle."

She sat up in the middle of the bed, lean and almost boyish-looking with small firm breasts, tipped by broad dark nipples. Her hair was blue-black with a deep prismatic sheen. The small triangle of hair between her legs was the same shade, disciplined and neat in its boundaries. "Where did you go?" she asked. "You just disappeared in the middle of the night."

"Out," he said, feeling disoriented. "I had to go out." He wondered what the other ego had wanted in the middle of the dangerous night. No matter, the thing had over a period of time assumed almost a consciousness of self as though in setting up the sequestered complex long ago in Pelambang, he had given it some sense of identity and capability for growth. It was a weird kind of vampire existence, he told himself, this assuming for moments or days the body of another man, even if he had created that man.

He came to the bed and looked down at her, marveling at her slim beauty. The body he wore was patterned after that of a man of thirty, hardly into his majority, and he felt the strangeness of being young and vital again with a woman like her.

"Elen," he said softly, "I'm sorry to awaken you."

"I'm glad you did," she said, crossing over to the edge of the bed as he sat down on the cold sheets. "We can be together so rarely."

"I wish it could be more frequent," he said.

She wrinkled her nose solemnly. "You know that I shouldn't even be seeing you. It's completely against the rules."

"Oh, damn the rules," he said violently.

"The rules are the rules," she said.

"You know what I think of such arrangements," he said.

"You could come back, be a part of us. I'm sure they'd all be pleased with you."

"Metafamilies are unnatural," he said angrily. "The whole concept goes against my nature."

"That one may love more than one person?" she asked. "I love them as much as I love you."

"I want you for myself," he said fiercely.

"Yet you won't give me all of you," she accused. "Oh, I know you say you would, but I know there's much more to your life than you will ever tell me. I've seen the way at times you change, seem a completely different person."

"I don't know what you mean," he said.

"Like now," she challenged. "You seem completely different from the man I went to bed with, somehow less joyous, older and more tired."

"That's just a part of me," he said, feeling as though he had just been unmasked.

"No it isn't," she said. "I know you very well now. This isn't the part of the you I know; it's something different, more frightening."

"More frightening?"

"Yes," she said slowly. "You've always frightened

me, you know. Ever since the night that we met in the park. I suppose that's why I asked you to take me home. I wanted to find out what frightened me, perhaps meet the fear and get over it . . . or conquer it."

"Instead," he said, attempting to be gallant, "you conquered me."

Her mood volatilized in the instant. "Oh, that's the one I like, not that cold gray man you were a minute ago."

He thought, I can't take this. Why did I ever start it? Did I need this phantom life, just because I sit somewhere far above and slowly die with no hold on life and manhood? Better return to the task at hand.

She giggled coquettishly. "Let's make love," she said, inching on her belly toward him.

"It's morning," he said.

"What a wonderful time for love," she said, and twined her arms around his surrogate thighs. He felt no passion, no arousal, only a faint sadness as she began to do special things.

Enough of it, he thought bitterly. This is not the time for seeking pablum for a damaged ego.

He had one brief glimpse of her great black eyes, wide and questioning before he cut the circuit and restored the automatic. Let her make love to a machine, he thought; it's surely no worse than I.

Then he was back on the plateau in the body he had so lately abandoned, wondering if anyone had noted his brief absence. Hardly twenty minutes had passed, he noted. Twenty minutes that might have been critical, but for that twenty minutes the tensions and the fear had dissipated, only to be replaced by . . .

He shook aside the mood and looked about him. He looked out over the plateau on which he stood. The control station, built on the truncated top of the "Needle," a massive volcanic splinter thrust up from the polar plain, was an organized confusion of cables buried in fused rock, complex instrument banks, and control consoles. Actually, once countdown had started, the station functioned strictly as a monitor. Automatic units in a control capsule buried in a pit on the plain initiated the transmission, directed the stream of plasmoids that was the Artery upward at the proper angle, and controlled the density and orientation of the magnetic lens generated by the orbiting lens stations two and a half million miles sunward in Pluto's warped orbital plane.

He turned his eyes downward, scanning the polar plain from the base of the jagged stone tower of the control station outward. His eyes paused on the bottomless crevice that ringed the stone outcropping like a ragged moat, then moved outward through the jet shadows that striped the irregular plain toward the sprawling units of the Artery. His gaze took in the vast curve of the accelerator itself, the glowing stokers, storage towers for their product, the great ionization towers. He itemized proudly all the vitals of the Artery that, like a vast creature rising from the dead rock, stretched its octopoidal arms over the polar region. Those arms stretched far south via the great conveyors to suck the very substance of the planet from the continental beds of uranium hydride. Below him the vast complex finally turned it into the pulsing blue beam that would hurl sunward in a few short hours.

The whole panorama, with its eerie half lights and strange brilliances, was something compounded of the fire and brimstone of the Christian hell of his childhood. Plato, with its endless stretches of centuries-old snow and blackness, which filled the vacuum plains and airless mountains like some yeasty dough in colorless ferment when they first came, had changed from a Norse hell to a Christian hell. It had become a place of raw energies where a creature of flesh and blood could not survive an instant, where the very space was laced with surging magnetic fields that would rip a man's body fluids to their component gases in seconds. Where the alpha and beta particles from the power pile, accelerated to near light speeds where their vectors coincided with the accelerator fields, would blast a fatal path of ionization through animal tissue, regardless of the shielding.

Yes, he thought, they had indeed turned it into a Christian hell, a thing like the warped images from some medieval heretic, shivering in anticipation of fire and brimstone. Not that it made too much difference, he thought. No man could live an instant here. Were there any part of him that owned the weakness of flesh and blood or carried a deadly dependence on protein and body fluid, he would cease to exist in an instant.

Steel, he thought, looking down at his thick metal torso and seeing the radiation from the generator making power in his vitals, *to live in hell you have to be a man of steel.*

For a moment he looked up into the black sky, seeing the stars, and wondering how much more one must be to go there.

Chapter Two

H MINUS THREE HOURS

The radiance below the Black Field Station has softened now. It has much the quality of the soft pearl light that comes from a well-functioning glow panel with just a trace of blue. The periodicity has increased slightly. McDow on the Commo Bridge observes it and wonders. He shrugs finally, assuming that the phenomenon, while unusual, is not alarming. The Research Survey Group will be back the week after the Artery has stabilized. They will undoubtedly be interested in it, but he thinks little of supplementing their observations with any of his own. He is much too busy with the communication manifold required by the complex activities of the Artery. In addition to the complexities of the Shrenk harnesses on board, he must maintain the tape that monitored the other transmissions from Earthside. Only a few of the Shrenk robots on Pluto have their primaries on board the Black Field Station. Most of the workers, with the exception of Chang, are based around the Earth, their transmissions relayed by one of several special communication satellites where line-of-sight transmission was masked. In addition, he is busy now with the five hundred channel transmissions that serve the various control and instrumentation facilities of the Artery with data computations and feedback corrections from the mammoth holography memory bank of the Pelambang computer. He has little time to wonder at the pulsing blue-white light that radiates in a narrow beam within the Black Field.

The snow had begun just at dusk and, as Akira Fusaka limped down the village street toward the tourist compound, he shivered, wondering if the spring would ever come. He had hated northern Hokkaido the first year he was assigned here, but in times of emergency one does not question. The snows of southern Honshu, his familiar home, were soft and rarely drifted to more than a few feet. Here in Hokkaido the snow was a vicious white animal that piled up against the compound, and no amount of heat from the charcoal braziers or gasoline heaters could completely take the biting chill from the air. He wondered at the urgency that had caused Kawakami-san to send for him so late in the day. The aging Ainu chieftain rarely ventured out after dark, preferring to stay in his fused-earth hut, surrounded by his children and his withered wife, who was one of the few remaining women with the anachronistic heavily tattooed lips.

Akira Fusaka wished that he had not signed for another period. He had been offered the choice of a more comfortable administrative assignment in the Marshalls, but the fascination of his research into the near-vanished customs of the Ainu aborigines had decided him. In spite of his dislike for the severe winters, he had elected to stay another year. Besides, his quarters were comfortable enough: a hut of packed earth divided into four rooms, one quadrant holding his small heater and power source, the others hanging with the furs the Ainu prepared and dyed for export. Indeed, he had more space at the station than he would ever have commanded in any of the southern metropolitan areas with their wartime shortages. They were probably more comfortable quarters than he could have found in the Marshalls, which were still primitive and disorganized.

He had recently moved his researches to Ezo Island, primarily because of the rumors that several of the Ainu in that area still practiced the bear ceremonies. He planned later that spring to go to Shikotan if his supervisors permitted, but for the moment the winters made that quite out of the question. He wasn't too sure, in any event, that he would find many uncontaminated remnants of the Kurile Island culture. The cultural shock accompanying the transfer of the Kurile Island Ainu to Shikotan in 1884 had very nearly destroyed that vigorous primitive culture. In the middle of the twentieth century, their numbers on Shikotan had dwindled to barely fifty. The basic culture that had been imported from the Kurile Island home had become attenuated during the near-extinction of the clan. It was a sad tribute to the Yamoto peoples that through the centuries this vigorous agricultural people had suffered such a marked decline while their customs and ways had steadily been modified and vitiated by the Japanese influences from the south. In the first part of the twenty-first century only fragments were left, mostly among the tribesmen who now practiced their ancient dances and ceremonies for the monied tourists from the southern islands.

He paused at Kawakami's hut, feeling the ache from his old leg wound, and bowed to the carved posts that marked the graves of his parents in the yard nearby. The grave posts were elaborately carved with pointed heads for the males and rounded heads for the females. In recent years the Ainu of the village had renewed their interest in the wood carvings of their ancestors, and one could in the village store buy some handsome *ikupashui* sticks, carved with the sacred bear figures and swimming kinapo sunfish. The designs were traditional, and it mattered little to visitors that these modern saké sticks were carved with power tools rather than with the ancient hand tools.

He entered the enclosed anteroom, removed his outer boots, and pushed aside the hanging after announcing himself to the hidden presences in the inner room. Kawakami was sitting before the Treasure Corner with his wife Yudiko, who was quietly weaving a *kina*. The bullrush mat blossomed rapidly from her skilled hands, and she did not falter as she looked up. Her upper lip was heavily tattooed in blue, so that in the dim light she seemed to be open-mouthed at Fusaka's presence. Near at hand, on a worn *tatami*, sat Kawakami's grandson, Kenjiro, impatiently picking at the loose straw on the mat. He was repeating a singsong recitation slowly as Kawakami listened.

The old man signaled and the boy fell silent as Kawakami rose and bowed to the visitor. Fusaka noted idly that the old man had recently removed the *kamidana* shelf with its miniature Shinto shrine, and he wondered what this signified. Surely not a rejection of his ancestors. The old man had behaved oddly in the past year, almost as if he were regressing to an earlier age as senility approached.

"My poor house is yours, Fusaka-san," the old man said and spread his hands. He glared at the boy at his feet and said, "We will continue tomorrow."

The boy scurried away. Kawakami said, "The youth, how disappointing they are. I learned the *Ainu yukar* at my father's feet proudly, long before *Genpuku*, the coming of age. Our children care nothing for the old epic chants."

He gestured for Fusaka to follow him across the room and seated himself on a pre-eminent chair, signaling Fusaka to take the honored right-hand chair position. Yudiko scurried away and returned with a small tray with saké and cups from which the carved saké sticks protruded. She served the hot wine and Fusaka sat, savoring the warmth of the drink in his hand as they made the ritual sips.

"You have wondered," the old man said abruptly, "what concerns me so late this evening."

Fusaka covered his surprise at the directness of the speech and nodded silently.

"It is the time for the festival of the bear," Kawakami said.

"That is true," Fusaka said.

"But who is it that may these terrible days find the god for *Kamui Omande?*"

Fusaka noted the formal word for the bear festival. At other times Kawakami would have simply used the term *Iomande*. He seemed somehow in an exalted mood, his face bright and suddenly excited.

"Who indeed?" Fusaka said, bowing his head.

"Our people had lost so much of the past that only occasionally do we raise the small god for the festival. The finding of one in the wilds is rare indeed."

"It is to be believed," the old man said. "This evening. It took many of our men to capture it and two were badly injured."

"Why did you not call me?" Fusaka demanded.

"But I have called you," the old man said, rising. "Come, we will display ourselves to the god together."

He stroked his full beard and rose slowly to his feet, the sleeves of his robe falling back to display silvered wrists. Fusaka marveled at the hairiness of these people once more. In spite of the centuries of crossbreeding with the Asian races, they still displayed this uncouth hirsuteness together with eyes that were in many instances quite Caucasian. He knew, of course, that even their blood prothrombin was distinctly Caucasian rather than Oriental.

The Ainu chieftain threw a heavy fur mantle over his silk-trimmed linen robes and beckoned for Fusaka to follow. Fusaka did so at a respectable distance as they left the hut and walked down the packed snow of the compound, their feet making soft crunching sounds in the white.

"The god appeared to us only this night and we captured him not without some injury," the Ainu was saying. "Tomorrow we will build the log fall between whose jaws the god will die. His flesh will be sweet upon our lips as we savor his godhood."

They were outside the compound now and approaching a small grove of willows. A massive cagelike construction bulked large against the snow-flecked trees. As they drew close, Fusaka saw that it was indeed a cage, a monster of a cage nearly ten feet tall and built of stout lashed timbers. He had never seen one that large, even in the days when the tribe still sacrificed full-grown bears that they thmselves had raised from cubs.

"It is the god indeed," Kawakami said, gesturing.

Fusaka leaned forward but could see nothing. He pressed against the cage and looked in. It was quite empty.

"Your god has flown, I'm afraid, old man," he said, stifling the urge to laugh.

"Only for a few seconds," the old man said. "It is like that with this sort of god."

A sudden roar of incredible violence reached Fusaka's ears. He had turned to address the old man and was totally unprepared for the sudden black thing that loomed in the darkness of the cage. Great razor claws ripped out at him, cutting flesh from his arm and tearing into the robe that covered his chest. He fell back in shock, staring at the blood welling from his front. A centimeter closer and it would have been no mere surface wound.

He stared in wonder and disbelief at the great raging beast that filled the cage and battered at the stout limbs that confined it. It was well over ten feet high and must have weighed over six thousand kilos. It was enormous, a black furry thing of foam-flecked teeth, great raking claws, and a blunt feral muzzle that grunted and hissed and snapped at its confining cage.

"By the gods, themselves," Fusaka said, stanching the flow of blood from his wounded chest. "It can't be anything else. A thing that died off the face of this earth eons ago."

"It is the great god of them all," the old Ainu said.

"A cave bear," Fusaka gasped.

"Must I?" Adrianne Patel said tiredly. Her olive Eurasian features gleamed slickly in the soft pastels of the overhead glow panels. She rubbed at her cheek self-consciously and frowned. She had always tended to an oily skin, and in moments of fatigue the fine-grained texture of her skin felt slick and cold under her fingers.

"I think it's important," Councilman Gilchrist said. "If I didn't think it important, I wouldn't ask it."

"But why in person?" she asked. "Why not by Shrenk harness?"

The councilman paced to the far wall and activated the polarized window. The muted purple of the sun-lighted scene lightened. Outside, the bright high-rises of New York gleamed cleanly. It took several moments to see the subtle signs of decay and atmospheric corrosion that had attacked their limestone cornices and metal fixtures over the years. Even many of the nearer buildings showed long corrosion streaks where the wash of summer rains and melting fall snows had carried dissolved metallic salts down their faces.

"Adrianne, Adrianne," Gilchrist said softly, "it's been over ten years. Surely that's all finished."

"You mean Norman, of course," she said. "I don't know if it's finished or not. Norman Bayerd is a proud man. For him I suppose it was finished the day I appeared before your committee and took issue with his schemes."

"Have you changed your mind?" Gilchrist asked.

"No, of course not," she said. "I wouldn't be helping you if I did. I don't like some of your methods . . . you know that . . . but I still believe the Artery was a terrible, terrible mistake."

Gilchrist turned and looked sternly at her. "Methods?" he countered. "You use whatever method is necessary to counter an attack. Simple morality doesn't count when you've got the fate of a society at stake."

"I suppose you're right," she said. "But everything seems like a personal attack against Norm, himself, and I can't help but be sorry for that."

"Now, listen to me," Gilchrist said, coming over to her and grasping her wrists. Standing over her, he looked down into her brown-black eyes. "You cannot weaken. There's little time enough to do what we must do. Soon our every bit of energy will be channeled to simple survival. Then we will have no time to look for alternates to the Artery. I don't care what you feel for this man. You must understand that he has made the Artery a symbol of his own ego, his own manhood. He no longer thinks rationally about it. For him the destruction of the Artery is something akin to castration."

She nodded silently, husbanding her special knowledge. To the personality that was Norman Bayerd, certainly the destruction of the Artery would represent a form of castration. You had to have been . . . still be, she told herself sadly . . . in love with a man to appreciate how deeply his ego and his concept of virility ran. Virility, manhood, she thought. It had no meaning any more. Love, well, that still had meaning. You do not fall in love with a man, she told herself. You fall in love with an image, a gestalt. Even if the man dies, the gestalt remains, preserved like some mystic hologram to be the unanswering recipient of emotion.

"You've got to put it out of your mind," Gilchrist was saying. "He is nothing but a man with a dangerous idea. You know where your duty lies, surely?"

"Duty?" she said with a bitter smile. "Do we always have to sacrifice meaning in life for duty?"

"Very frequently," Gilchrist said. For a moment his

hard, forbidding face softened, and he touched her on the shoulder lightly.

Why, she thought, you are concerned for me? I have always viewed you as a sort of political juggernaut, grinding your opponents and your allies alike under your wheels.

Strange, she thought, the depths of compassion one finds in the most unlikely of men.

Night had descended on Pelambang with the quiet intensity of the tropics. In another time the sky would have been ablaze with the crystal brilliance of stars while the horizon would have reflected the intense gegenschein of the latitude. That was long ago, Karl van der Reis mused as he stood on the rooftop of the Artery Computer Complex. Years ago before Pelambang had grown to the sprawling mass of modern buildings and decaying slums, years before the night skies were silted over with the perceptual fog from the reactor heatsinks on the lesser islands, the night sky must have been breathtaking.

He had grown tired of the endless bickering below amid the quiet panic of preparation as the time for the reopening of the Artery approached. So many small minds, obsessed with the paper details of the bureaucracy that infested this place, the last emotional stronghold he had found on a teeming, stink-drenched Earth.

He was scarcely aware of another presence for some moments after Martin came from below. The younger man stood silently, respecting his solitude until he took notice. He turned and smiled at Martin, thinking that he was maturing most handsomely. Martin was a member of van der Reis's metafamily, and he had been delighted when Gerta and Carmelita had decided to add him to the group. He and Carmelita were the two youngest members, but surprisingly, they rarely cared to cohabit with each other.

"Karl," Martin said, "we just received word from the station. Commander Bayerd is shrenking down for a final tour in fifteen minutes."

Van der Reis shrugged. "Well, is there anything that needs to be done? He's a pretty hard taskmaster at times."

"I don't think so," Martin said, his ruddy face broadening with pleasure. "You look very tired."

"I am," van der Reis said. "This is a very critical period. I don't think many of us will get our full night's sleep for the next forty-eight hours."

"Carmelita isn't back yet," Martin said at length.

Van der Reis frowned. "That's quite unlike her," he said. "Have you contacted Manila?"

"Yes," Martin said. "She went north to visit her brother yesterday in Dagupan. They haven't heard from her since."

"Let's see," van der Reis said. "She's with the Muletti group, isn't she? They'll need her for the final calibration pulse later this evening. You'd better get a tracer out for her. We can always call Imir back, but he's ill and I would prefer someone who isn't distracted by a malaise."

Martin nodded silently and turned to go. At the last moment, he stopped and turned. "I'll be glad to get home tomorrow," he said.

"So will I," Martin said, blushing.

"For that reason too," van der Reis said. The boy

retreated in confusion down the staircase. Charming, van der Reis thought, and dismissed him from his mind.

He found a cigar in his jacket and puffed it alight as he spent his last minutes of freedom, looking out over the city in silent contemplation.

His ancestors had come to these islands long ago, their raw Dutch muscles prying a reluctant fortune from the plantations and later from the shipping along the north seaboard. They had lost most of their wealth during the Sukarno regime in the fifties. A new generation in the seventies and eighties had found a unique role in the burgeoning technology of this, one of the new noncommitted nations. The island republic had made itself an independent technical bastion, servicing the small nations who themselves could not afford the complex gargantuan research establishments of the great powers.

Yet, in spite of several generations in the Indies, van der Reis still thought of himself as Dutch. His wispy dark blond hair, already thinning in the crown at thirty-five, confirmed that ancient European heritage even though the flatness of his face and the slight trace of a Mongoloid fold testified to the later racial admixtures that had modified his genetic heritage. He was still, as his father before him, very much a European. His mind followed Western pragmatic patterns in spite of the trace of Oriental mysticism inherited from his Chinese grandmother and the animal restlessness of his Polynesian cousins, who had always chafed at the physical restrictions of the white man's civilization.

In the midst of the final countdown, he had suddenly felt the need of cold air on his face. He had transferred control to his second, a stolid, plodding Australian named (appropriately) Means, and had sought the rooftop of the twenty-storied, air-conditioned, static-desensitized building. Now he stood, drawing on a forbidden rum-soaked Havana crook, and stared out over the city. To the south he saw the flickering of man-made lightning, the discharges in the basic sugar synthesizers. Pelambang was one of the centers of basic sugar synthesis because of the proximity of the reactors; the electricity was a must to the synthesizer tasks of coupling formaldehyde and methane generated from wastes collected throughout the South Pacific into the simple trioses that were later upgraded into pentoses and hexoses to supply the insatiable maws of a dozen hungry nations in the area. It was far more efficient than the growth of beets and sugar cane, since it took the energy of the process from the most compact source available to man, the energy of a nuclear reaction.

He was somewhat concerned at the absence of Carmelita. It was quite unlike her. She had been a member of his metafamily for four years now, and he had come to know her moods and her strengths as well as his own, indeed as well as he knew the intricacies of the psychology of Martin, Fuad, Gerta, and Liat, the other members of the family. You do not cohabit with five other people for from one to ten years without coming almost to the point of telepathy. He conjured a mental vision of her . . . long, jet-black hair, perfect olive complexion, somewhat full lips, a slender, lithesome figure with small but perfect breasts and, surprisingly for her Irish-Spanish ancestry, a very small, almost sparse triangle of pubic hair of blue-black brilliance. He and Gerta and she had cohabited just the week before, the night before she went on her vacation, and he remembered the subtle physical and emotional interplay with pleasure. He chided himself at playing favorites within the group. That was always a danger, of course, just as now Martin seemed to have developed a special bias toward him. Of course, the boy was still young, and the young tended at times to be selfish, but . . .

His lapel communicator beeped at him and he said, "Van der Reis."

"We have the carrier wave from the station," the voice said.

"I'll be right down," he promised and cut the transmitter. He turned for one last look at the city. In the distance a soft glow on the horizon brightened and flickered. Another fire, he thought. There had been a great many fires in the past three weeks, often in quite inaccessible spots with no clear rationale for their beginning. This fire, he saw, must be in the garment district. The flammable solvents in that area would give the fire fighters a great deal of trouble. He had a mental image of the vats of thermoplastic material bursting and their contents flowing into the streets. That sort of thing had happened two weeks ago in one of the casting plants, and the casting metal had run in molten rivulets into the streets, cutting down the fire fighters as they stood. He shuddered at the memory of the sequences on the late-night news. It seems almost as if high-energy points were appearing spontaneously within the city and starting fires. There were other similar situations abroad he knew, although his work had been too time-consuming to allow him to follow the news that closely. He dimly remembered a fire in the top floor of the Cyborg Trust Building in

South New York. The problems of battling a blaze in the top floor of the world's tallest building had been insurmountable, and the top twenty floors of the building had been finally abandoned. Fortunately, when the spire toppled it had fallen northward. The building was on the edge of the modern construction that marched with monomaniacal insistence up to the edge of the crater of the '96 burst. As a result, only a few structures were in the path of the flaming debris and shattered stone and plastic that cascaded from the skies.

He stepped onto the levitator belt and descended into the building, sinking slowly through thirty floors to the programming complex. In the anteroom, he donned his black robes and nonreflecting mask, carefully avoiding the walls of the room since these still occasionally shed microcontaminants onto the clothing in spite of their most severe efforts to keep the place free. The black robes were, of course, important, since he would probably move among the holograph memory banks during his tour, and any stray reflection into the banks of fluorescent foam that formed the transient memory of the computer would, if it did not erase or destroy a trace, certainly reduce the redundancy in that one sector to a point that might be critical to full accuracy.

The room beyond the anteroom was a long ribbon of quiet discipline, with technicians moving down past 'cord-out stations, keying steps in the model sequences with pencil lights focused to almost microscopic beams, playing intricate chords upon the inductance surfaces that programmed the machines beyond the room. Occasionally, someone would cut in the audio on his programming bank, and theraminlike music would drift eerily over the bustling sounds of the room as skilled hands manipulated programming sequences.

Martin was waiting for van der Reis, his youthful face shrouded in a black gauze, his lean athletic body bulking large in the black robe that he wore.

"Has he arrived yet?" van der Reis asked.

"The carrier wave is on," Martin said, indicating the red tag on a bank near the ceiling.

They walked swiftly back to the Shrenk chamber and as the door slid silently aside for them, the manlike shape in one corner seemed to shake itself awake and rise from its resting position.

"Norm," van der Reis said. "Are you in control?"

"Of course I'm in control," the voice said. The shape stepped forward, moving haltingly at first and then with a sureness. It was quite humanoid although a bit tall, slightly over two meters in height. On the street, van der Reis thought, no one would know that it were not human except for the height, which in itself was not unusual. Not at least except in an Asian city, where the men tended to be ten or so centimeters shorter. His own European ancestry had given him an unusual height, although Bayerd's alter ego now towered over him by a good five centimeters.

"I thought I'd give your installation one final check," Bayerd said.

Van der Reis grimaced. Surely the man should know by now that little was to be gained by this. Let him tend to his engineering and leave the computer section to someone who knew the intricacies of modern digital machines.

"Good," he said, not meaning it at all. "I'll show you through the program."

"All right," Bayerd said. "Then I'd like to talk with you in private."

"Martin is my metaspouse," van der Reis said.

The robot Bayerd made a slight face. He did not, van der Reis remembered, approve of that sort of arrangement. "I would prefer it to be quite alone," he said.

"Very well," van der Reis said and ushered him through the door of the Shrenk chamber, Martin bringing up the rear.

They toured the programming room quickly. This was nothing new to Bayerd, although the programming stations had grown in complexity since the last time he had been here nearly a year before. Finally, van der Reis said, "Would you like to see the new memory banks?"

"Are they in operation yet?" Bayerd asked.

"Not for another fifteen days," van der Reis said. "You won't need special optical protection."

"Fifteen days? We could use them tomorrow," Bayerd said, the faintest hint of annoyance invading his tone.

Van der Reis wished that the man wouldn't be so impatient. That was something that his personality could well do without. That irascibility, ill-contained though it was at times, was probably a reflection of the drive that had made Bayerd a driving creative force. Could van der Reis have tampered with the complex programming of that brain, he would not have attempted it for fear that he might destroy the very thing that made Bayerd the giant that he was in this power-starved world.

"The foam matrices were installed just two days ago," van der Reis said as they descended the levitator shaft to a spot three floors below the programming room. The corridors in this area were walled and floored with foam and acoustically deadened by heterodyning generators so that one could only talk by pressing one's mouth close to the other man's ear. At a distance of a foot, all sound was canceled by a directionless beam of countersound from one of the generators along the chamber.

They walked silently toward the matrix hall, where transparent columns of optically active foam towered for three floors. The foam was dead now, and they would walk easily between the columns with no thought of optical shielding or of X-ray burns from the scanning systems. Lights reflecting from the surface of Bayerd's body brought echoing phosphorescence from an adjacent column. Van der Reis's own optically neutral body did not bring an accompanying echo.

"They're a hell of a lot more complex than the last installation," Bayerd said.

"The new plastic is much more optically transparent," van der Reis said. "That means we can store bits to a depth of twenty meters, whereas before, ten to twelve meters was the limiting diameter of our matrix."

The great columns were filled with a foamed polyester, each closed cell being little over one micron in diameter. The general effect was a high column of milky material that was only slightly translucent. However, the system was perfectly transparent to the X-ray scanning beams that carried the information to the matrix. The depth of penetration depended on the wave length of the scanning beam, and each bubble stored energy for approximately two seconds, before emitting it to a photosensitive system within the matrix. The end result was a two-second temporary memory capable of storing an enormous number of bits, and accepting those bits at multiples of light speeds. The angle of the transmitter could be manipulated at such a rapid rate that the transfer of a transmitting beam from one microcell to another was at the apparent speed of five light units, from one extreme end of the column to another.

Bayerd stood silently, looking up at the great columns. "You know this is all completely lost on me," he said at last.

"I thought you might want to see them," van der Reis said with a faint annoyance.

"I know that. I didn't come down here to pretend to supervise you," Bayerd said, turning on him. "You're one of the finest talents in your field."

"Then why?" van der Reis said, eying the massive figure. He wondered what must be going through that distant mind with its fascinatingly complex personality. Not even Bayerd recognized how well van der Reis knew that space-locked ego. Perhaps no one but a select few about him would ever really know just how much the complexity of the personality that was Norman Bayerd was known to a few like van der Reis.

"To be honest," Bayerd said, "I suppose you could ascribe it to a sort of voiceless anxiety. I'm concerned and perhaps a little bit afraid."

Van der Reis raised an eyebrow. That, he thought, was certainly a confession he would not have expected from this monolithic man.

"We can handle the new transmission," van der Reis assured him.

"Even fifty years from now?" Bayerd asked.

"That's the purpose of the new units," van der Reis said. "The control demands, of course, become more and more critical as Pluto approaches aphelion, but our technology is equal to it or will be."

"Then this isn't the final solution?" Bayerd asked.

"No," van der Reis said, shaking his head. "We're pushing our recall and storage technology now, but we have fifty years ahead of us, fifty years of growth and sophistication. When the need finally becomes acute, we will have the technology."

"I sincerely hope so," Bayerd said tiredly. He seemed to shake the massive body and then said, "Can we go someplace and talk?"

Van der Reis eyed Martin and shrugged. "My quarters," he suggested. "Perhaps some wine. . . ." and then he stopped and laughed a short barking laugh.

"It *is* deceptive," Bayerd said with faint amusement, gesturing at the body he wore.

"One tends to forget," van der Reis admitted.

"There is even provision for taking on food and drink," Bayerd said, "but it seems a shame to waste your good wine."

"Well, come ahead," van der Reis said and led the way back through the halls to the levitator.

Van der Reis's installation quarters were a miniature reflection of his home in the city, small and comfortable without ostentation except for a single small Chagall on the far wall, a lithograph of faded brilliance in purples and greens of a peasant, his wife and a cow floating at odd angles in a lavender night sky over a central European village through which a small group of people followed a bent rabbi.

Van der Reis gestured for Bayerd to take a seat and

eyed him in indecision. "I'm concerned about the recent observations I mentioned earlier," Bayerd said at length. "Have your people been able to do anything on the model I suggested?"

"The tachyon model?" van der Reis said. "It seems very farfetched, Norm."

"I know it, damn it, but offer me a better approach. We've been shunting the kinetic energy of the beam into the Black Field for forty years and we still haven't accounted for the major portion of it. The tachyon emission during deceleration offers the clue perhaps. I'm concerned that we understand this phenomenon before we proceed many more years."

"You removed the research team, cut them off from our facilities," van der Reis reminded him.

"Simply because they weren't doing anything. The approach they are following is a complete dead end."

"How can you know?" van der Reis challenged.

Bayerd's surrogate head furrowed in momentary confusion. Then he said, "I don't know. Call it intuition. Call it what you wish, but I'm sure in my bones that they are wrong. Can you understand that? The certainty without knowing quite why."

Van der Reis nodded, thinking that he, of all people, could probably better understand this than even Bayerd. The rationale was obvious to him, even if it were not to the other man. Of course, this was not something you could put into words. Better accept it as face value, as simple intuition. . . .

"I can trust this," he said slowly. "If you feel that it's the wrong approach, well . . . I've learned to trust your intuitions before."

"Thank you," Bayerd said. For a moment the stern visage melted in an expression of such humanity that van der Reis was touched in spite of himself. The subtleties of the robot face amazed him. In it he could see the fatigue mirrored in Bayard's real face, the sense of uncertainty to be disguised with the intense drive, the overwhelming ego of the man. Then the moment had passed and the man-robot was again monolithic, untouchable by human emotion.

Remembering Lady Macbeth, van der Reis thought inanely, I would not have such a heart in my bosom for the dignity of the whole body.

The heart? The brain? The personality? He thought wryly that in spite of the ancient words, he did indeed in a sense have the heart that went with dignity of the body. It was a frightening responsibility, he told himself. He felt that silent emotion that Bayerd always inspired in him.

"I must get back," Bayerd said. "I'm expecting visitors," he added wryly.

"So soon?" van der Reis asked. "I would have expected that they would leave you alone during this critical period."

"I wish they would," the man said tiredly. "It's bad enough without the tensions here on Earth and every petty eye looking over your shoulder. I feel completely hemmed in sometimes. If it weren't for the alter egos," he gestured at the Shrenk body, "I think I'd go quietly out of my mind. At least I can still participate in mankind."

He shrugged and his lips twisted in bitterness. "At least vicariously," he said.

After Bayerd had left, van der Reis busied himself for some minutes with the model Bayerd had discussed. It was much too complex for his talents, he decided, and thought at length that Martin certainly had the background to pursue it. He must be very careful with Martin, however. There were things that not even Martin could know, and in giving him access to that series of memory banks, he came perilously close to compromising information that had for years been the most closely guarded secret of the center. Well, no matter. It had to be done and he would face the other problem when it arose.

He was still musing on this problem when the intercom spoke in his ear and he was told that Carmelita had returned. Not returned. Rather she had been brought back. "She's in the No. 5 dispensary under sedation," the secretary said. "She wants to see you."

He felt a sudden alarm at the news. He had been subconsciously worried for most of the evening, for it was quite unlike her to be late. Of all the members of his staff, she was certainly one of the most conscientious. Besides this, she was acutely aware of their special relationship and took great care not to presume upon it. He put aside the report he had been browsing through and hurried down to the dispensary on the first level. Martin was outside waiting for him.

"What's wrong?" he asked.

"I'm not sure," Martin said. He looked worried, his young face flushed with excitement. "They brought her in by 'copter about fifteen minutes ago. She made her way back to Dagupan and insisted they bring her here immediately. Her brother is apparently fairly potent in that area. He commandeered a trawler and had her flown back."

"Yes," van der Reis said absently, "he's a district tech leader. He could do that."

"Two of his rangers found her on the Dagupan

road in a state of shock. Apparently her machine had left the road and overturned."

"That wouldn't affect her that much," van der Reis said. "She's much too level-headed for that."

The door opened and Lemaelle, the shift physician, came out. "Good," he said, seeing van der Reis. "She's been asking for you. She's in the damnedest state of hysteria I've seen. She keeps raving about losing her head."

"Literally?" van der Reis asked.

"Literally," Lamaelle said. "I won't tell you what she told me. It's too improbable. If I didn't know her at all well, I would say that she's the victim of a long-standing systematic hallucination."

"Can we see her?" Martin asked.

"I suppose so," Lamaelle said. "Yes, I think it would do her good."

He gestured for them to follow him and entered the dispensary. They walked along quietly lighted halls and stopped at a door. "Just don't excite her any more," he cautioned. "I'd rather you didn't ask questions or talk about what's disturbing her. We'll get to that later."

"All right," van der Reis said and they entered the small room.

She looked quite small in the hospital bed, van der Reis thought. Small and very pale. Her eyes flickered open as they approached and for a second a frantic look of disorientation flickered in her eyes before she identified them. She half sat up and said,

"Oh, Karl."

He was at her side in a minute, holding her slim form. She was quite pale under her natural olive color and when he touched her, she began to shiver uncontrollably. Martin came to the other side of the bed. He leaned over and kissed her lightly on the forehead. She reached out to clutch his hand impulsively.

What, Karl wondered, could have frightened the girl so much?

Chapter Three

H MINUS TWO HOURS

He was floating in space, the afterimages of the Pelambang Station still dancing in his mind. Where a moment before, his limbs were clothed in steel and plastic, throbbing with an unnatural energy, he was now a flesh-and-blood man, enclosed intimately in the pantographic harness of the Shrenk transmitter on the "S" level of the Black Field Station. He pulled his face from the all-enveloping mask that had touched it, following each facial muscle to give the illusion of humanity to the robot below. He cut the transmission, knowing that in that moment his far body had become lifeless and cold, untenanted.

It took a moment for his eyes to become accustomed to the darkness. Phosphenes danced across his vision. One of them seemed to quiver, grow larger. It were as if he were looking down an infinitely long tunnel, watching a human figure swim toward him. Not swim exactly, but drift with the kind of movement a drowned man has under water. It was not illusion, he realized. The drifting motion was perfectly normal in an area of free fall. The man figure was not. There was simply no stretch of distance that could give such a perspective. The walls of the chamber were too close. Yet, it appeared as if he were a hundred yards or more away, drifting slowly toward Bayerd.

He tried to focus and saw that it was a very young face. The eyes were wide and startled but very knowing. It was as if he had launched himself out into the no-gravity blackness and were surprised that he did indeed float even while he knew that he must. His face, Bayerd realized, looked very familiar and he wondered who he was. Certainly no one he knew on the station, but the station complement had grown so in the last month that he might well be mistaken.

In the next instant the man figure vanished. It were as if someone had pulled a switch, cutting the light to a projection. One moment the figure was drifting toward him and then there was no figure. The afterimage persisted, and Bayerd realized that the figure had been brightly illuminated. The sudden blackness surprised him. Where, he thought, had the light come from? The figure was mystery enough, but. . . .

He felt a sudden chill at the thought that he might have imagined it all. It was not a comforting thought.

He heard the quiet sound of a door rising. He touched the induction spot by his arm, and soft radiance filled the room. The illusion of distance dissipated in the instant, and he was again amid familiar surroundings. He floated from the harness as McDow propelled himself from the hatchway and said,

"Norm, are you all right?"

"Of course," he said, somewhat irritably. "What makes you think I'm not?"

"You've been working very hard," McDow said. "I think you should take better care of yourself."

"I'm not exactly an invalid," he said and then laughed bitterly. "No, that's not true. Of course, I am. I forget that on Earth I would be little more than a basket case."

"That's not what I meant," the other man said. "You ought to have Doc Beckwith give you a thorough going-over."

"Doc fusses with me enough as it is," Bayerd said, rubbing his hand across his forehead and noting the faint perspiration that wetted his fingers. "Have our guests arrived yet?" he asked.

"They're below at station center," McDow said. "I wanted to catch you before we started the circus." He handed Bayerd a message flimsy.

"What's this?" Bayerd asked.

"I checked Commo just before our guests arrived. You know, the usual routine of checking the log against the morning transmissions. This one wasn't entered."

"Looks like a communication code," Bayerd said, scanning the sheet.

"It's not one of our routine codes," McDow said. "Can't make it out. If I hadn't been running a spot check, it would probably have been erased from the tape automatically at the watch change."

"I don't like this coming on the heels of Gilchrist's arrival," Bayerd said slowly.

"Do you think Gilchrist might have an agent in the station personnel?"

"You know these men better than I do. What's your idea?"

"Doc Beckworth, Chang, Girard, Muletti, Trubner, Sanchez," McDow said, checking them off slowly, "no, I can't see any of them working for Gilchrist. Maybe one of the group we had here during changeover."

"Whoever sent this message," Bayerd said tiredly, "probably knows there are only eight of us physically left on the station. That's fairly common knowledge. If there's a plant, he's still here. Otherwise the message wouldn't have been sent."

He folded the message and placed it in the pocket of his tunic. "You get back to our visiting firemen," he told McDow. "I have a few things to do before I join you."

"Very well," McDow said and left.

As soon as the door closed, Bayerd found an anchor on the low case of the Shrenk unit's oscillator and sat breathing heavily. Thank heavens, he thought, McDow left when he did. He felt the throbbing in his temples and the pain at the base of his skull from the old injury. He found the vial of capsules the doctor had given him and took one. Without water, the capsule made a hard lump in his throat and he sat for several minutes after the lump had faded, waiting for the lax calm to steal over him, waiting for strength to ooze into his tired muscles. Finally he mounted his chair and guided it on silent jets down the long corridor lined with Shrenk unit cubicles, most of them now unused, to one of the tubes leading downward toward the center of the station.

The center of the Black Field Station was a hollow sphere, nearly five hundred meters in diameter, laced with silver cables like the traceries of a careless monster spider, and cut by fragile catwalks thrown up with no apparent regard for "up" until one realized that "up" was away from the center of the hollow sphere. Quite apart from the hollow interior's function as an auxiliary station in the Black Field, it served a somewhat more frivolous purpose, needing darkness.

Here he was in free fall and he was able to leave the prosthetic chair. He pushed from his seat and found one of the catwalks in the darkness.

He anchored himself to one of the cables in the darkness without a sound. He could hear a murmur of voices and he saw vague man-size blobs of darkness floating near the center of the sphere, their forms outlined by the light from the projection on the walls that enclosed them.

For a moment he felt a secret thrill at the vast panorama spread across the darkness. Not even death, he thought, could be frightening with such a thing to leave behind him. For the first time in the last hour he felt better, more secure. To hell with the Gilchrists of the world, he thought. A hundred years from now, when the Artery still blazed across Earth's night sky, who would remember *them?*

Even after years of familiarity, the illusion was breathtaking. It were as if he were floating in space with a blazing wealth of stars surrounding him. Then the sense of disproportion grew as he saw that he was viewing the Solar System out of scale from a vantage point above the plane of the ecliptic. The sun was unnaturally small, and far out the exaggerated point of light that was Pluto moved. Beyond Pluto, massive Charon moved in its eccentric orbit, inclined a full sixty degrees to the plane of the ecliptic.

From Pluto's displacement in relation to the ecliptic, he decided that the time was just past perihelion but before Pluto had crossed Neptune's orbit. That marked the time as just before the turn of the millennium. He could understand McDow's reasons for picking this period rather than one more recent.

He watched as Pluto enlarged for the instant that Artery transmission began. A brilliant ribbon of blue, swirling with suntines of pulsing green, darted from the point of light upward at an angle and then bent sharply to parallel the ecliptic as it touched the field of the Alpha Orbital Lens inside Pluto's eccentric orbit. The lens was microscopic on this scale but the image enlarged for an instant to show the five lens stations revolving around a common center while the incredibly dense magnetic field that they generated within their mutual circle warped the beaded beam of the Artery from its original path.

The ribbon of cobalt light traced its path slowly toward the sun, curving in opposition to the planetary motions of Pluto and the Earth, its velocity a pedestrian quarter the speed of light. The increasing radiation pressure of the sun was making itself felt as the beam passed the orbits of Jupiter and Mars, introducing a new distorting influence upon the beam.

The tiny image of the Earth-moon system enlarged now, the moon trailed by the tiny Nodal Plane Lens Station in its metastable orbit. The beam, almost at Earth's orbit but well displaced above the ecliptic, touched something in its path and disappeared. Whatever the interfering object was, it did not scatter the beam, but the blue streamer emerged from the area at a snail's crawl, as though in some fashion it had shed most of its quarter-of-light velocity.

"At this point," McDow's voice cut the darkness, "the major portion of the beam's kinetic energy has been absorbed by the Black Field. It then passes through the Earth Orbital Lens, is deflected downward through the Nodal Plane Lens that trails Luna to the plating surfaces on the moon."

"Humph," a voice rumbled, "why get rid of all that energy? Needless waste."

"If we didn't, Councilman, we'd probably melt down a good hunk of the moon during the course of operations, not to mention losing most of the transmitted metal by reflection."

The glowing beam, scarcely moving, intersected the Earth Orbital Lens and turned sharply down toward the ecliptic. It was showing a tendency to spread now as it slowly approached and touched the Nodal Plane Lens. There was a moment of suspense as the lens redirected the beam perpendicularly to Luna's surface and it crept slowly toward contact. The blue radiance touched the surface of the moon, flared faintly, and contact was made. The two worlds, Pluto and Luna, were joined in a thin band of glowing U-235 plasmoids, a pulsing umbilical cord of ions.

"Marvelous," Committeeman Mendoza's voice said from the darkness. "Like Archimedes and his lever."

"Marvelous?" the harsh voice said. "So was the dinosaur."

"Lights," McDow said, and the interior of the station was suddenly flooded with brilliance.

Bayerd freed his line and pulled himself across the intervening distance to the five figures who were floating in random orientations in the center of the station. Beckworth, the station's M.D., was holding the small control box from whose side a thin cable snaked up to the projector positioned on one of the catwalks.

"The dinosaur was a necessary evolutionary step, Mr. Gilchrist," Bayerd said.

"You know Commander Bayerd?" Mendoza said, his nervous white smile punctuating his dark skin. Bayerd frowned quite without realizing it. The faintly unctuous tone of the dark man always annoyed him a bit, although he was happy enough to have his political support. It was the general feeling that here was a man who would be trusted only so far as personal advantage took him.

"We've met," Gilchrist said in a rumbling voice. He was big . . . well over two meters, with a kind of monolithic massiveness only lately turning to fat. For all of his decaying beefiness, he gave the image of a physically powerful man. Such men, Bayerd thought, never actually decay through the years; rather they seem to come apart physically almost in an afternoon. Gilchrist tossed his huge head with the faintest touch of wattles, his fringe of yellowish-white hair floating in the zero gravity about the shiny bald pate as though it were something no more substantial than a haze of yellow-white light.

"We have indeed met," Gilchrist repeated. "At those endless committee hearings . . . was it? . . . twenty years ago. God, it seems almost yesterday."

"Not for me," Bayerd said.

Gilchrist eyed his floating figure as though realizing suddenly that he was forever bound in a gravity field to some prosthetic device. He colored and said, "Well, of course, many things have changed."

"The essentials never change," Bayerd said fiercely, feeling an unreasoning anger. The man was trying to be polite, but Bayerd felt the surge of annoyance nevertheless. He could see that Gilchrist was annoyed also by his manner.

"I think there's someone else here you'll enjoy seeing again," Gilchrist said. "Adrianne, come here and say 'Hello' nicely to the man." He turned and beckoned to a dark figure floating somewhat to the rear of the group.

She floated forward easily, her large liquid eyes glistening. It had been years since Bayerd had seen her; yet it was suddenly as if only yesterday. He would have recognized her anywhere . . . in the most crowded of thoroughfares she had changed so little. Except for a touch of furrow in the forehead, a faint tissue thinness to the flesh around the eyes, she was as untouched by time as that aching bright autumn day years ago.

"Hello, Norman," she said. "It's good to see you again."

Bayerd nodded, not trusting himself to speak. He felt a quick warmth on his face and wondered at the sudden sense of confusion, the quick feeling of welcome and joy followed by a flood of remorse and then anger. Anger, he thought. He seemed to be able to respond to no situation these days except with quick anger. Somehow he brought his inner rage under control.

Bayerd checked his chronometer and said, "We have ninety minutes to beam time, Councilman. McDow will show you and your party to the Shrenk units assigned you if you've finished here. I presume you've all had experience in handling the pantographs?"

"I think so," Mendoza said. "I haven't handled one for a year, but they're relatively simple."

Gilchrist sniffed. "Like wearing a second skin," he said. "It's a pity we can't watch the operation in person."

"That's the last thing you'd want to do," Bayerd said wryly. "It would be hard to find a more inhospitable planet than Pluto even before we set up the Artery operation. Quite apart from the surface gravity and lack of atmosphere, the radiation level from the uranium hexahydride beds is pretty bad. Mostly alphas and gammas, of course, but awfully difficult to shield against in an articulated suit. We're pretty convinced now that the planet as we know it is really the planetary core of a rover that the system captured. The gravitation stresses pulled the mantle away and scattered it as debris between Jupiter and Mars. That high density coupled with the peculiar albedo had the astronomers of the last fifty years in a quandary."

"There will be alternate units for each of you," McDow interjected. "You may key a robot on the plain or on the Needle during the operation."

"Good," Gilchrist said sourly. "I want to get a good look at this dinosaur of yours."

McDow turned and led the way toward one of the personnel tubes. Bayerd floated slowly in the same position as the group moved out. He was unaware that Adrianne Patel had stayed behind until he heard her voice near his ear.

"It is good to see you again, Norman," she said.

"Is it, Patel?" he said.

"Patel, now?" she snapped impatiently. "Patel,

Patel, so formal, so proper, so goddamn free of any human emotion."

"I haven't had any real human emotion except impatience for a long time," he said.

"So proud . . . the great wounded lion," she said. Then, "I'm sorry. I have no right to poke at you."

"No, you don't," he said. "You have no right at all."

She paused, tried to reply, and then blinked rapidly in the half dark. He ignored the response, ignored the faint stirring of compassion in his own thoughts and waited silently. After a moment she said, "Perhaps we can talk later. It seems such a shame that we can't talk."

"Yes, doesn't it," he said. In spite of the cruelty and irony of the words, a part of him thought that it was indeed a shame, indeed too bad that they had found themselves so unalterably apart.

After she left, he drifted to the spot where he had anchored his chair and moved slowly down the mesh leading to the personnel tube. Mendoza was waiting for him at the entrance of the tube.

"Norm, unbend a little," he said softly. "It's been a great many years."

"Toward her? Toward Adrianne Patel?" he asked slowly. "It's not a question of unbending; it's just that you can say so much to each other, so wound each other that the time comes when the response is purely automatic."

"Watch your step, nevertheless," Mendoza said slowly. "Gilchrist is up to something, I'm sure. I don't know if Patel is involved but we all need the best allies we can find at a time like this."

"When did she get on Gilchrist's bandwagon?" he

asked. "I wasn't even aware that she had been active politically since the last confrontation over the Artery."

"Gilchrist hired her as a private consultant for his committee during the hearings earlier this year when the power crisis became acute."

Bayerd snorted impatiently. "That political hack," he said.

"No," Mendoza said. "He's bullheaded and about as singleminded as they come but give the devil his due. He wants a way out as badly as we do. If the Artery is truly the solution, he'll accept it, but Patel and the rest have convinced him that this may well be the wrong way to go."

"We decided that long ago. We committed all of our energies to this approach years ago."

"Are you satisfied we were right?" Mendoza asked.

"Of course," Bayerd said. "What a question. Is there any doubt of it?"

"I have my doubts some time," Mendoza admitted.

"Then why do you continue to back the appropriation?"

"Do we really have any choice at this point?" Mendoza asked. "As you say, we've committed all of our energies to this solution, and it seems to me that there is little turning back." He turned to go, and Bayerd reached out to delay him.

"Before you go," he said, "can you tell me if you have anyone spotted in my crew?"

"What do you mean?"

Bayerd told him about the message in the unauthorized code.

"That seems strange," Mendoza said slowly. "I suppose it might be an agent planted by Gilchrist or one of the individual districts involved in the census dispute, but to what end I can't imagine. Perhaps they're tying to demonstrate that part of the Artery fissionables can be diverted."

"Whatever the situation," Bayerd said slowly, "I don't like it. The Artery should be above politics. It's too vital to the survival of our whole culture."

"Read your history, Norm," Mendoza said wryly. "Nothing is ever above politics."

Chapter Four

H MINUS ONE HOUR

In the last hour before countdown van der Reis found little time to think about Carmelita and her story. His mind was busy with a thousand small details and with a task that was readily evident even to the members of his staff at the Pelambang Station. It was this latter duty that occupied him in the last minutes before the great memory units were activated and the scanners rechecked out.

He left the main part of the station and dropped four floors to a part of the station to which only he had access. Here the walks were surfaced with a light-scattering compound and the floors deeply carpeted with an antistatic surface. His own optical robes were tightly drawn as he moved through the silent corridors to a spot where a single seat rested before a grill set in a wall. Below this grill a single induction plate for fundamental programming response gleamed a dull copper in the reddish light.

He sat in the chair with a deep sigh, and his black gloved hand drifted over part of the induction panel, activating the response mechanism on the other side of the wall. There was a voder and voice copher that operated through the mesh grill. He sat, listening to an endless *sotto voce* response from the machine beyond, nodding occasionally as potential levels and capacitance values changed under his quiet ministrations.

I wonder, he thought to himself at one point, if ever a single man in history has held such power?

It was a rather frightening and yet a very prideful thing to van der Reis, even though it was unlikely that other than a select few would ever know this part of his function. Still, to be trusted to such a degree, to have such a function thrust upon him. . . .

Norm, he thought, Norm, old and dear friend, would you be outraged . . . grateful? It mattered little enough. One did what one had to do to keep the great sprawling mechanism of human society alive and working, and if it required the most incredible of compromises . . . still, one did what one must. For duty and, he thought wryly, for love.

He leaned forward, his chin in his hands listening to the faint whisper of the voder, quite unaware of his surroundings until . . .

The presence of the man announced itself in a faint whisper of displaced air. One moment he was not there and the next he was.

"And is this the confessional, priest?" the man said in the faintest wisp of a voice, his tone bitter.

He was a young man, lean and athletic-looking, with a saturnine cast to his features. Van der Reis tried to focus on his face, but it seemed somehow indistinct, wavering. This annoyed him as much as the man coming into this area unauthorized with no sign of an optical suit, a thing strictly forbidden.

He cut the programming pickup and demanded, "What are you doing here?"

The other man said nothing.

"You have no business here," van der Reis said fiercely. "I'll have you on report for this."

The man smiled wanly and turned. He seemed to be walking away as van der Reis watched. His figure dwindled, receded into the distance, and disappeared. Beyond him was the short nonreflecting corridor. Wherever he had disappeared, it was not along the corridor to the levitator.

Van der Reis shook his head, his anger disappearing in puzzlement. Finally, not knowing what else to do, he turned again to his task. Just before he activated the programming plate, he thought wryly that in his black optically inactive suit seated before the spartan wall with its single plate and grill, he did rather look like some ancient priest hearing confession.

The simile, he realized, was much more accurate than he would have preferred. . . .

In the last half hour before countdown, Bayerd ignored the visiting party. He could not, however, completely dismiss them from his mind, particularly Adrianne, whose sudden appearance had opened memories that he had felt buried forever. The presence of the others was an ill-perceived threat hanging over his head. That they should have chosen to come during this critical period was ominous, and he knew that the others involved in the changeover would be affected by the thought that the Earthside party was both figuratively and literally looking over their shoulders. He wished again that the changeover might have been delayed another year, but he knew he was only running away from a more fundamental problem.

Besides, there was the other factor of his age. Sixty was hardly old in this day of advanced gerontology, when men were accustomed to living a vigorous and socially potent life to well past one hundred. In his case, however, the slow advance of his particular medical problem more and more robbed him of even the basic muscular strength he needed to maneuver about the station. In the past five years he had seen the steady decline of strength and reflexes until now he must confine himself to the prosthetic chair in every part of the station except the zero-g areas. On Earth he would be a complete invalid, but here, fortunately, he could still lead a useful and generally ambulatory life. Every time, however, that he returned from one of his strong metal selfs on Pluto or on Earth (and most especially from the one particular most secret self that few knew about in New York) to the flesh-and-blood shell in the station, he felt as if he had crossed from the living to the other than living. The vicarious life of the Shrenk robots gave him a new and separate life, knowing that on that world on far Pluto or in the teeming dank cities on the Earth below he was alive. Knowing that there on Pluto existed a world he had built, complete, conceived by him and executed with the last vital energy of his personality, a part of him that would collapse into the rubble of history and be forgotten if he faltered and such vandals as Gilchrist prevailed.

Ever since Pluto had passed out of Neptune's orbit after perigee in 1989, it had moved in a path more and more displaced below the ecliptic. The eccentricity and inclination of the orbit had changed Pluto's orientation to the ecliptic all the while its distance from the Earth had increased. The problem of control had grown greater and greater as the beam, originally parallel to and displaced above the ecliptic, now cut through the plane of the ecliptic for its contact with the Black Field and Earth Orbital Lens.

The changeover had become imperative after the turn of the millennium. It had taken the engineering team six months to change the positions of the two lenses and the Black Field, jockeying the fragile stations in a broad path perpendicular to the ecliptic while still maintaining their proper motions. During the period, of course, the Artery could not transmit, and the Earth's fissionable reserves had steadily dwindled, forcing an even tighter rationing than that which prevailed when the beam was in operation.

Fortunately, the rationing system was already well established. Terrestrial power demands had caught up with the new supply of fissionables from the Artery scarcely five years after the beam was in operation, and rationing on a complicated formula weighing both population and industrial development had been the only answer. The political situation had been tense before the changeover, but tempers had flared again in the World Council and threatened to explode in open violence over the week-old scandal following the discovery of the attempt to falsify the count in the Liechtenstein District during the current census.

In the last minutes before final checkout, Bayerd remained on the plain away from the group on the control point. After he had checked the vapor tower of the main smelter and the grid temperatures of the first bank of ionization chambers, he moved across the plain and out of the accelerator to the control capsule. The ceramic shield that covered the electric winch, which would lower the capsule into its hundred-foot pit in the rock, had been stripped half away, and the faceplate and remote visual pickup that scanned the capsule instruments had been moved back on their gimbals to facilitate the final adjustment of the capsule mechanism. Once the controls had been set and locked on the capsule, it controlled the widespread functioning of the units within the accelerator circle by a dozen coaxial cables buried deep in the rock as well as the orientation and density of the Plutonian lens. A signal from the Needle could override the capsule and cut the beam, but the capsule and the massive computers buried beneath the plain handled the actual transmission at speeds impossible to an organic nervous system. Once the Artery was in operation, only the capsule site was accessible. The raging magnetic fields near the accelerator would completely destroy control of a Shrenk robot. The capsule would transmit an initial calibrating segment of the beam and then twenty hours later make any necessary adjustments from data fed back to it by the Earth Orbital Lens Stations and begin continuous transmission.

He paused by the capsule and looked out over the plain, feeling his inner self fill with pride. What a magnificent concept. Without the Artery they would still be chasing the pot of gold at the end of the rainbow, as Adrianne Patel had wanted them. Patel and her single-minded search for a new power source. You couldn't harness the hydrogen reaction, that had been proven. What else were there but the old standbys, uranium and plutonium fission? With the 20 percent conversion you got with the Black Field, that meant a lot. When the vast beds of U-235-rich ore had been found on Pluto, the power famine on Earth and in her ambitious colonies had been critical. It was commercially impractical to bring the metal back by ship. The drain on world resources of merely building the ships would have been fantastic. The Artery had been a heaven-sent solution to the dilemma. Who cared how much energy you burned at the source? So smelt the ore on Pluto, vaporize it, raise the vapor to an ionizing temperature and squirt out the cloud of ions and electrons, shape them with electromagnetic pulses, bite them into small chunks of plasma with internal particles rotating fast enough to organize them into those almost-living cohesive clouds of particles called plasmoids, accelerate them endlessly in a giant accelerator until they reach nearly a quarter the speed of light, and hurl them sunward so that twenty hours later you plate out precious metal on the lunar plains.

That was the concept, ready-made, a mere matter of engineering, complex engineering to be sure, but the technology already existed. No striking into *terra incognita.* They couldn't wait for the vain hopes of a new power source, nor was there enough to back that expensive phase of research and still build the Artery. A choice had to be made.

They built the Artery.

If there had been any sense at home, Bayerd thought, the power would have been enough for centuries. It wasn't his fault that industry and power usage had expanded so rapidly to meet the new supply. The point was that he'd given them what they wanted, and in the process had built the greatest structure man had ever conceived.

He checked the time quickly and called "Check in!"

"Trubner. Ionization chamber full potential."

"Girard, how about smelters?" Bayerd asked.

"Intake full idle. Reservoirs at 90 percent."

"Field stability?"

"Sanchez here. Accelerator field oh point oh oh five variation at reserve."

Quickly he took the reports from Muletti's crew at the far side of the accelerator below the horizon and from Chang, whose men were running a final remote check on the computers far below. He checked the settings on the capsule once more, made sure the screws were tight on the verniers, and said, "Trubner, grab Girard's crew and get the capsule sealed and seated. . . . Gentlemen, ten minutes to countdown."

He watched figures detach themselves from the shadows about the blue-hazed ionization chambers and move toward him. For an instant the scene seemed unreal, as though he were displaced miles from the site. He shook away the sensation, stepped back a pace, and deactivated the robot. A brief adjustment and he was in the alternate robot atop the Needle, feeling somehow vaguely depressed after the surging emotions of the plain.

There were three active robot bodies and, when he switched to the normally unused "B" net, he heard McDow explaining the functioning of the metering stations while Mendoza and Gilchrist occasionally made comments. He started to break in on the conversation when one of the three inactive bodies standing on the far edge of the arc straightened and moved toward him.

Bayerd turned to look out over the tableland below, trying to ignore the robot that he knew must be Adrianne. He switched to the "A" net to rid himself of the three-way conversation between McDow and the councilman. Below him the whole plain was aglow with energy, except for the deep fossa ringing the base of the Needle as a moat rings a castle, cutting it from menace.

"It *is* magnificent," Adrianne said quietly.

"The culmination of every engineering technique since the pyramids," Bayerd said.

"With something of the attributes of them," she said.

When Bayerd did not answer, she asked at last, "Have you ever read Shelley's 'Ozymandias'?"

For seconds Bayerd struggled with the anger surging within him. McDow's voice cut into his thoughts: "Norm! Three minutes."

He switched to the command net and moved quickly to his station at the accelerator monitor, where flickering meters told of the varying potentials below and the prognosticated azimuth of the beam on transmission. McDow took his position at the console that monitored feedback information from the Plutonian Lens as the others withdrew and waited silently. McDow keyed the warning signal, waited thirty seconds, and then checked to see that the team below had withdrawn.

"Thirty seconds," Bayerd announced as the timing light on his board glowed. "We are now on automatic."

The twenty-second light glowed on Bayerd's board

as McDow took up the countdown. Impatiently Bayerd lowered the volume and thought, *A minute from now and it's ended. Only Patel and Gilchrist left, and their fangs pulled.*

Like mice nibbling at the feet of a steel colossus.

"Fifteen seconds," McDow announced tensely.

"Lens checkout."

"Computer reading forty-five two three two."

"Orbital lens?"

"One thirty-four . . . thirty-six . . . fifty-eight."

"Check." Bayerd released the override switch. The countdown began as a taped voice said, "Ten, nine, eight . . ."

He checked his own readings again. Right on the nose. The beam would strike the lens at just the right angle and arrow its way sunward. The Artery would be whole again in just twenty hours.

"Three . . . two . . . one . . . zero!"

"Look, look!" He heard a quick intake of breath from someone on the net as the three visitors peered upward at the band of pale blue springing from below the horizon and piercing the sky. Bayerd switched to ultraviolet vision, and the beam blazed as though a giant brush, dipped in liquid fire, had been raked across the sky. Below it, the space above the smelters was a riot of swirling color like a phosphorescent oil slick on black water, as secondary radiation excited the escaping hydrogen and painted the sky with Geissler colors.

The group was lost in the sudden wonder of it, and he could only stand and drink in the beauty spread across the sky. Only in the last instant did he hear McDow shout,

"My God, cut it!"

Automatically his hand lashed out for the override switch. Something arced within the console, and sudden brilliance bloomed on the plain below. An invisible sponge wiped the colors from the sky.

"Something happened," McDow said. "The angle was wrong at the lens."

"Did you stop it?" Bayerd demanded.

"I managed to before the board went dead."

"Did you stop the whole transmission?" Bayerd demanded.

"Almost all," McDow said. "All but about a thousand-meter segment."

"Will somebody explain what happened," Gilchrist demanded.

"The transmission was wild," Bayerd said. "There's a thousand-meter segment of the beam heading sunward."

"Heading for where? The lens . . . dead space . . . what?"

"Councilman," Bayerd said, feeling a constriction in his throat, "I wish I knew."

Chapter Five

H PLUS TWO HOURS

"How could it have happened?" McDow asked quietly. The only sign of his inner turmoil was the beading of perspiration on his pate and forehead. "What could have gone wrong?"

Bayerd looked out over the deserted metering bridge of the Black Field Station, and shook his head. He sank back tiredly into the prosthetic chair, feeling tired and suddenly quite old. "I don't know," he said. "The monitoring board was calibrated just an hour before. I saw the operation myself and it checked against the primary generator standard to plus or minus point oh-oh one percent."

"It just simply could not have happened," McDow said.

"But it did," Bayerd reminded him. "Something went badly wrong, so badly that the system arced and fused the cable that supported the capsule."

"Any word from the crew yet on what happened?" McDow asked.

"No," Bayerd said. "The shield was badly damaged; that much is apparent. They'll have to cut through it before they can raise the capsule. What I'm really concerned about is the speed with which van der Reis can give us results from the Pelambang computers. It's a pity the new units aren't yet in operation. That would have speeded results by an hour."

"They've had the data for two hours now," McDow pointed out. "I don't know that the saving of an hour would make that much difference."

"It may make a hell of a difference," Bayerd said irritably. Then he wiped his hand across his head and said, "I'm sorry, Terry. The tensions of the past few days are just beginning to get to me. I hadn't realized how keyed up I was until the moment the transmission started."

"You drive yourself too much," McDow said sympathetically. "After all, you have to conserve your strength. The results will come soon enough."

"We can't do a damned thing until they do come," Bayerd snapped irritably. "Chances are, of course, that the beam will cut through the system without incident and head into interstellar space. There's a great deal of free volume in the system compared with the volume occupied by planetary bodies or ships. The odds are all against it."

"Of course they are," McDow said.

"But," Bayerd pointed out slowly, "we were transmitting toward the Earth-moon system. Our computer directions were designed to intersect the plane of the ecliptic at just that point. If the misdirection is only minor, we may well strike the surface of the moon directly. . . ."

McDow shuddered. "We'll have to evacuate the Mare crews if that's so," he said. "I'd hate to be around when that much kinetic energy is unloaded in one spot."

Bayerd moved his chair restlessly across the bridge to one of the monitoring screens that looked out from the Black Field Station. Idly his hands drifted over the induction switches on the panel before him. The screen flickered and became alive. The view was from one of the lens stations. Against the blackness of space, the points of light that were the other five lens stations formed a new constellation moving slowly in concert around a common carrier.

To the pickup the stations were perfectly stationary. It was the star-flecked backdrop of space that seemed to revolve counterclockwise about the fixed constellation. Separated somewhat and at a great distance, Bayerd could see the five subsidiary stations that generated the Black Field forming a second constellation of bright points with the slightly brighter sixth point, the Master Black Field Station, from which the field was propagated and from which he presently viewed the total panorama. It was an odd sensation, watching the point of light that was his present position as it glowed coldly in the revolving night sky . . . rather like the illusion, Bayerd thought, of the picture of a man looking at the picture of a man looking at the picture of a man and so on down to the infinitely small. The "Pet Milk can" illusion they called it, although the reference was obscure to him.

"I'm concerned," Bayerd said at last. "The arrival of Gilchrist and Patel . . ." He hesitated. He had almost said Adrianne, but his lips refused the syllables. "The arrival of those two followed by the coded message and then the beam failure. It seems more than coincidence."

"Don't jump to conclusions, Norm," McDow protested. "Coincidences *do* happen, you know."

"You're probably right," Bayerd said with a small shrug. "I'm letting my own personal dislikes lead me into all sorts of suspicions." He smiled wryly. "The first exercise of the incipient paranoid personality."

"Well, everyone is paranoid to some extent," McDow said. "The nature of a strong ego is to personalize every opposition."

"Thanks for the vote of confidence," Bayerd said, smiling in spite of himself.

"Any time," McDow said, mounting a light ladder and disappearing through a ceiling port. Bayerd watched him go, thinking how much he had grown to depend on the whimsical Irishman with his unpredictable sense of humor. He could be as dour as a judge and then suddenly full of vivacity and daring, his eyes twinkling with merriment. An unpredictable personality but certainly an attractive one.

He debated going below for a nap, then chided himself at how easily he still fell into the parlance of the planet dweller in his thinking. "Below" to a planet dweller meant, of course, toward the center of gravity. Automatically you began to think of "below" in a station as toward the center of the station, forgetting that the "gravity" you worked under in a station was actually centrifugal force from the spin of the station, and that as you traveled toward the center of the spherical station, the force of this pseudo-gravity dropped until at the exact center of rotation, you were completely weightless.

But you didn't revise your thinking on such basic terms. You still held to the old patterns of thought, mostly because it was easier, because you didn't want to stop each time you used a direction oriented to a gravity field and decide the correct term. "Below" and "down" were always toward the center of the station but in exactly the opposite direction, toward the outer shell when you were talking in terms other than that of movement between levels. It did make, he thought, for some odd contradictions.

He guided his chair across the bridge, intending to take the vertical shute to his quarters. The scuffling of a foot behind him startled him, and he touched the controls for the side jet, whirling his chair uncontrollably. It took him a quick moment of panic to bring it under control. He turned to see Adrianne coming from the passage that McDow had lately ascended.

"Do you usually move around so silently?" he snapped. "You caused me quite a turn for a moment."

"I'm sorry," she said. "I wanted to come down and see if you'd calculated the new beam path yet."

"No," Bayerd said. "We've transmitted the data Earthside, but our analogue machines aren't capable of handling such a wide variation. We'd had to put it on the digitals, and the program is slow without the new memory banks."

"I know," she said. "You may recall that I did a statistical analysis of the performance of the analogue servomachines several years ago."

"A rather self-seeking piece of work as I recall," he said bitterly.

She stared at him, her large brown eyes sorrow-filled. Finally she said, "Does it always have to come to this? Can't we find some area of civilized exchange so that we aren't constantly cutting at each other's flesh?"

"The present situation is not one of my choosing," he reminded her.

"Nor of mine," she said. "I wish to whatever gods we both believe in that I could have seen it your way, that I could be on your side in this, but I think you've been blinded by a personal vision that has become so hopelessly entangled with your personal image of mortality and virility that . . ."

"Oh, spare me your amateur psychoanalysis," he snapped irritably. "If you have nothing more valuable than that to contribute, I'll leave. I need the rest."

"Norm, Norm," she said, "I wish I could believe, but I think you're terribly wrong."

"As you have demonstrated," Bayerd accused.

"As I have demonstrated," she agreed.

"Without the Artery," Bayerd said, turning back to the metering board, "there'd be no fissionables today.

You know what that means. We'd have slipped back to a level of technology that would never have supported space travel or the world's population."

"Perhaps," she said, "but you haven't done the world any favor. I remember when we first met and you had stars in your eyes when you talked about an interstellar drive. Well, you've shoved the human race into a straightjacket now, restricted it to this one second-rate sun simply because further growth is limited by the present supply of fissionables. We're spending a major portion of the world budget for operating the Artery in just maintaining the status quo. What happens if the Artery can't supply us with even the present fissionables? What happens if we have to fall back on some other resource?"

"Don't try to pretend that this accident threatens the existence of the Artery in any way," Bayerd snapped, turning to face her. "You'd like to believe that with this little malfunction, the Artery is through."

"If you believe that . . ."

"What I believe is not important," Bayerd said. "The Artery is my justification."

"And your monument."

"And my monument."

"To endure through the years," she said. "Only it won't endure through the years. The existence of the Artery is already practically at an end. Today is just a symptom of troubles to come."

"Today's accident was just that, an accident. Our control of the beam is normally damned good."

"Yes, your control is good, but will it always be?"

"What do you mean by that?"

"Just think about this for a moment," she said.

"Pluto is outside Neptune's orbit now and moving away from perigee. With an eccentricity of point two six, that means that its distance from the Earth will increase radically in the next decades. By the time it reaches apogee, it will be well over one and a half times as far from its conjunction with the Earth as at perigee in 1989."

"Do you think you're telling me something I don't know?"

"Perhaps you just haven't been willing to consider the implications. What's your feedback oscillation in initial transmission?"

"Less than one ten-thousandth of a second."

"What happens when the target subtends an angle less than that?"

"An undamped oscillation, but . . ."

"Go on," she challenged. "Calculate the probabilities. How many situations like today are going to arise in the next two decades? How long can you continue to operate under those conditions?"

"You can't convince anybody of that."

"Can't I? I can convince you if you'll think about it."

"Anything to destroy the Artery. It's a personal crusade with you. I wouldn't trust any calculations of yours to navigate across a deserted street."

"Because you distrust me? Or because you can't face the destruction of this massive symbol of ego?"

"Even if there were an element of truth in this, we're constantly improving our equipment," Bayerd said.

She shook her head.

"No, Norm, it won't work. You've put all of our eggs in this one basket. Our growth is geared to and limited by the fissionables from the Artery. In forty years, you'll have reached the point where you can't deliver. Even if you refine your equipment, there's a limit, and after that you can't hope to meet the control problem."

For van der Reis the two hours following the transmission failure had been like a nightmare. The data tapes from the analogue machines had given them the basic azimuth and transmission orientation data they needed, but the analogue devices themselves were capable of calculations and corrections of the beam orientation only within narrow limits. The circuit deviations were too great beyond a certain area to allow a reasonable extrapolation of the data. For this reason they had been forced to use the digital programs, and these were necessarily slow at the moment because of the partial loss of storage. The new banks, had they been operative, would have made all the difference.

He had already assigned Martin to the tachyon problem, and he hesitated to take him from this since he had already spent several hours in the first programming of the new model. At length he turned the initial programming of the beam transmission over to Means, who made a face and started automatically to work. Means was anything but an inspired and inventive worker. Short and squat with thick bristly fingers, he looked more like a day laborer than a computer man. He spoke rarely and in an odd cockney accent that belied his natural intelligence. Nevertheless, his intelligence was routine and uncreative, precisely the sort of mind needed for this type of work.

He returned to his office and after making several

calls contacted his counterpart in New York. They discussed at some length the problem of activating the new memory banks. Fenrenc in New York had been primarily responsible for their design, and he was able to offer some suggestions for shortcuts in activating them. By this time van der Reis was reasonably sure that they would need them within the next twenty-four hours. Fenrenc believed they could be brought to 75 percent capacity with some shortcuts in circuitry, but he would not vouch for the long-term damage to the installation if they were used in this manner. Van der Reis shrugged philosophically. It might be a matter of grave concern that these were put into action, so much so that they would willingly risk some damage to the units.

Fenrenc said that he hoped not, since they represented an enormous number of man-hours and might not be easily replaced in time for the next phase of Artery operation.

At length van der Reis cut the connection and sat feeling the sudden weight of his body. He had hoped to be able to go home by this time. The calibrating transmission would be on its way, and the next day they could get the final data for feedback to Pluto, and the continuous transmission could begin. The sudden emergency had canceled all of these plans.

He checked briefly with the dispensary and found that Carmelita was resting well. The doctor assured him that she could, if necessary, be depended on to assume her post within the next hour or two. He suggested, however, that she be allowed a full night's sleep.

Van der Reis sighed. He hoped that it would be so,

but a persistent intuition nagged at him. He thought briefly of his other problem, and wondered at the man who had interrupted him. It was a strange sort of apparition. There was no photo effect from the man's presence, almost as if he had been a mere projection and not truly there.

Odd. Especially in view of several other pieces of data he had been assembling over the past few weeks.

He was musing on the consequences of these when the communicator chimed softly. He keyed the communicator and said, "Yes?"

The man on the screen said, "I'm Chander of Metronews, Herr van der Reis."

"Oh, yes," van der Reis said cautiously. "I recall your being out here a week ago with several newsmen."

"That's right," Chander said. "I've heard a rumor of trouble out there and thought I would check with you."

"What sort of trouble?" van der Reis asked.

"Well, I'm not sure," Chander said. "We've heard that there's some problem with the Artery transmission."

"The Artery transmission isn't due to start for nearly thirty hours," van der Reis said.

"You should have transmitted the calibration pulse by now," the man on the communicator said.

"That's correct."

"Is everything in order then?"

"We don't have our results yet," van der Reis said. "You know that's the purpose of the calibration pulse."

"I thought your machines were pretty fast."

"They are," van der Reis lied. "However, we certainly wouldn't begin continuous transmission until the calibration section entered the lunar Black Field and we could get final fine data on the transmission."

"I see," the man said slowly. "Well, perhpas I've been misinformed."

"I think perhaps you have," van der Reis said and cut the connection.

"Damn," he said softly. If the rumor were out now, there would be all hell to pay. He must do everything possible to halt its spread until they had ascertained the nature of the transmission error. He called the P.R. office and gave quick instructions, knowing that he was probably already too late to prevent the first whispers of worry from trickling around the world with the speed of modern communication.

He must have dozed, for it was fifteen minutes later when the communicator again chimed. It was Means. "We're getting the first approximation printouts," he said slowly. "I think you should get down here."

"All right," van der Reis said, noting the faint play of emotion over the man's normally stolid face. He wondered what could be causing the concern. He dreaded finding out.

The intercom on the duty officer's desk chimed, and Bayerd turned his chair to the instrument. The screen mirrored McDow's worried face. Bayerd could see he was calling from Commo.

"Norm," he said, "are you alone?"

"Patel's here," Bayerd said.

"We've got the results from Earthside."

"Bring them to the bridge, will you?"

McDow nodded as his image faded from the screen. Bayerd waited silently, avoiding Adrianne's eyes. He moved to the hatch when he heard McDow ascending.

"Here," McDow said, breathing heavily. He handed Bayerd the flimsy pages with their dark brown markings.

"Never mind," Bayerd said. "What's the verdict?"

McDow pointed silently at the last page.

"Are they sure?" Bayerd said after a moment.

"It's a first approximation, but van der Reis thinks it's good."

"A one-in-a-million chance," Bayerd said, slapping the papers against his thigh.

"It could be a lot worse," McDow said.

"Or a lot better."

"What's the answer?" Patel said.

Bayerd handed her the sheets. McDow motioned to him and walked back to the hatch.

"Trubner's just reported on the capsule. They've got the shielding off," he said. "The cable suspending the capsule was severed by the arc. The capsule's still at the bottom of the well with a hundred pounds of melted metal debris from the short circuit on top. It may take two days to cut down to it."

"My God," Bayerd said, "and that thing is set to start transmitting the continuous beam twenty hours after the calibration pulse."

"Unless it's overridden."

"But the control circuits from the lookout are gone."

"But not the metering circuits."

"What good do they do?" Bayerd said disgustedly.

"None, but they gave us a picture of the capsule settings. The angular settings were way off. The set screws that lock the verniers were all loose."

"Norm," Adrianne Patel said behind them, "are they sure of these figures?" She pointed to the flimsies in his hand.

"They're sure," Bayerd said.

"Then the beam will tangent the Earth's upper atmosphere?"

Bayerd nodded silently. He turned to McDow and said, "Get down to Commo and contact lunar relay. Get data on every ship in space along the beam path. Also any available magnetic field generators that we might get shipborne within the next fifteen hours. Anything else that you can think of. We've got seventeen hours to either intercept or deflect that beam."

"What about the Pluto installation?" Adrianne asked.

"Get on it," Bayerd said, and McDow headed for the hatch. Then he whirled on the woman. "Don't worry. We'll get to the capsule before it's too late."

"If you don't, what then?"

"Perhaps you'd like to blow up the accelerator?"

"You may have to."

"You'd like that, wouldn't you?"

"No," she said. "I would not like that. We're too dependent upon the Artery . . . all of us."

"I'm surprised to hear you admit it."

"Why? It's obvious . . . but you know what happens when you cut an artery?"

"Huh?"

"When you cut an artery, Norman," she said with a worried frown, "you bleed to death."

Chapter Six

H PLUS FOUR HOURS

Slowly the dawn line flows westward. Now the first glints of the rising sun touch the spires of St. Stanislaus in Warzawa while to the south light flows like quicksilver across the Libyan desert, casting great rounded dune shadows before it. Still farther south Johannesburg, steaming with the acrid vapors of the sprawling chemical plants on the edge of the city, is already glowing yellow and red in the oblique rays of the rising sun.

Half a planet behind the dawn line, another line is moving. Rather not a line but an area expanding as the Earth rotates. Its beginning is in the foothills of Dagupan, where hours earlier Carmelita met briefly the strange beings from out of another time.

To the north on the edge of this expanding region at another time, Akira Fusaka found a troubled sleep. His lacerated chest still throbbed with pain under the bandages. He was sleeping in a warehouse on the edge of the compound, having committed himself with Kawakami-san to an all-night vigil near the great cage. Inside, the beast, roaring with a savagery unknown in this area for eons, flickered in and out of existence like a guttering candle. Fusaka turned in his sleep and frowned. A part of him dimly prayed that tomorrow would have exorcised this impossible demon, but he was afraid that it would not. In the meantime, he had radioed his observations to the prefectural headquarters and to his own superiors in Sugimotocho in Honshu. Hopefully he would receive some instructions by morning, assuming that his report would be noticed in these recent terrible days of fire and disaster.

The peculiar region had no clear borders. Rather it was an area of *influence*, expanding now to the Asian mainland. In the north, cold winds blew across the tundra of Tanu Tuva, and silent herds became suddenly restless, alerting sleeping herdsmen. Many awoke that night and spoke fearfully of shadowy horsemen racing phantom mounts across the night sky. Farther south, in the depths of the Cambodian jungles, vague figures shifted and stirred like errant shadows in the midst of the ancient limestone temples. The intricate bas-relief and carvings of the temples were now badly eroded and pitted by the acrid industrial fumes drifting in from nearby distillation and cracking towers, but in the mottled moonlight they suddenly took on a newness and integrity they had not had for centuries. Refinery workers in the area awoke to the distant sound of cymbals and gongs and drifting nasal chants. From the northern tundra to the southern jungles, the night had become haunted.

The region was expanding as well to the east, but most of the area was still in the Pacific Ocean. There were a few small island groups . . . the Marshalls, Solomons, and the like . . . but the peculiar phenomena within the area had not yet become too obvious to these static areas, where great plankton plantations policed by relatively few workers made up the main activities of the region. Had one tried at this point to plot the general extent of the area, one would have found it bounded by a relatively expanding circle. It appeared almost as if two spheres had tangented initially in the Philippine region and that the tangence had now continued to an intersection. When the intersection of the two spheres reached the size of a great circle, one might assume that the two spheres were completely congruent. The significance of such a congruency at this point was not clear.

Martin in Pelambang was thinking about such a congruency at that moment. In the midst of the excitement of the sudden beam emergency in far-off Pluto, Martin had continued on his initial assignment. He knew that van der Reis would have contacted him and returned him to the main activity if there had been need for his talents. Since there was not, he continued in one of the subsidiary areas to examine the data now coming in from several areas over the Pacific and the Asian mainland.

In addition to the data from Luzon (he had interviewed Carmelita at some length), he now had the first reports from Fusaka in Hokkaido, from several fisheries and floating processing plants in the China Seas, and he was now investigating earlier instances of apparent time phenomena. By this time, of course, he had identified the various improbable happenings as some sort of time lapse in the continuum that did not fit existing theories. It had become imperative, therefore, that he develop a more descriptive model in order to deal with the observations that he had. One thing Martin had become sure of and this one thing he explained to van der Reis when he looked in briefly.

"The whole thing is tied up in some fashion with the tachyon flux being generated by the Black Field Station," he said.

"Well, that's what Norman Bayerd assumed," van der Reis said, his thoughts elsewhere, on the immediate pressing problem of the Artery failure.

"If you examine the events of the past year, there are other isolated instances of phenomena similar to these."

"That I hadn't expected," van der Reis said.

"The isolated fires I mentioned earlier, for instance," Martin said. His young face became intense with the excitement of the problem. "There's some sort of energy flux appearing at apparently random areas on the face of the Earth. It may be basic to the phenomenon or it may be merely that the time effect is tapping some local energy source in time such as a fire or even a star located at these coordinates in the past or future."

Van der Reis shook his head. "This is quite beyond me," he admitted. "I'm not sure but what the existence of a tachyon itself isn't a bit too mystical for my blood. I grew up when it was assumed that no particle could travel faster than light in a vacuum. It was almost an article of faith with us. Einsteinian physics became almost a second religion to us."

Martin smiled absently. "Of course, I understand that," he said. "However, the Special Theory doesn't exclude the existence of the particle, provided it is created, traveling faster than light. It's the transition velocity that is excluded."

"Transition velocity?"

" 'C,' the velocity of light. A particle traveling below the speed of light may not be accelerated to the speed of light while a particle . . . a tachyon traveling faster than light may not be decelerated to the speed of light. In both instances the amount of energy required for the acceleration or deceleration would be without limit, that is infinite."

"That sounds like sheer black magic," van der Reis admitted. "However, I still don't understand how the simple existence of even such an impossible particle can result in the phenomena we're beginning to observe."

"Not impossible," Martin pointed out. "However, there are obvious consequences to the existence of a particle that comes into being at velocities greater than light. For instance, if there is an interaction and absorption of particle 'a' to yield product 'b' to one observer, the nature of the tachyon event is such that, to another observer, it would appear that the order of events were different, that the event was the adsorption of 'b' to yield a tachyon and particle 'a.' "

"Quite clearly impossible," van der Reis said tiredly. He had grown somewhat tired of Martin's didactic tone and wished he had not started the conversation.

"Not at all," the boy smiled. "What it does say is that we must view time as a series of completely formed world lines, that is, that all past, present, and future are forever fixed in some nether space as real lines."

"Nonsense," van der Reis snorted. "What you're telling me is that we can in proper perspective see time as another spatial dimension."

"I suppose you might view it that way," Martin admitted.

Van der Reis left him and proceeded along the deserted corridor, wondering at the impossible vision of himself forever fixed in another space like an insect in amber, his endless selves frozen in time. As Martin has said, of course, it was not a completely rigid scheme. The existence of the tachyon hinted at such an ordering of world-time lines, but it also offered the mechanism whereby events of the past or future might affect the present. It was such a theory upon which he and Bayerd had begun work, and the problem now was devising a self-consistent geometry to describe such a universe so that a computer model could be written.

He shook his head in wonder. This sort of study had always been beyond the emotional grasp of his more pragmatic and pedestrian mind. He could handle the elements of orbits and all of the permutations of planetary body interactions . . . that is, he could ask the proper questions and his machines could handle the problem. Here in Martin's study, just knowing what questions to ask was quite beyond him. He did know that the Black Field was now generating an unprecedented tachyon flux and that a large number of paranormal, presumably time-connected phenomena had been observed with increasing frequency during the past months. The significance of these made him shudder a bit.

He thought he would catch a short nap, certainly not over fifteen minutes. It was obvious that the night was going to be long, and he was already too fatigued to trust his sure judgment. He sought his quarters and spoke the word that dimmed the lights to a tolerable level. Then he lay back on his couch and pulled a light coverlet over him. Because of the perfect temperature and air control of the room, the coverlet wasn't necessary, but somehow the easy pressure on his chest and limbs gave him a kind of comfort. "Security blanket" he told himself drowsily, as his mind drifted into a controlled slumber. His last thoughts were briefly of the black figure that had accosted him in the inner computer area. A quick dart of chill touched his being. The computer station there was the most secretly guarded of all his responsibilities, and the ease with which the being had penetrated to that point was a nagging worry on the periphery of his mind as he lost consciousness.

"I've radioed Earth for complete information on all ships in space within the beam area or about to take off into the area," Bayerd said, scanning the faces of the men on the bridge. Only Chang's face was emotionless. His black eyes were lidded in thought, his face completely composed. The others—McDow, Adrianne, Dr. Beckworth, the two councilmen—showed varied expressions of worry and anger.

"Damn it," Gilchrist said, "we can't be worrying about ships in its path. We've got to divert that beam."

"Councilman," Bayerd snapped, "that's exactly what we're trying to do. But you need ships to move any equipment into the beam's path."

"What about the Black Field?" Gilchrist demanded. "Can you move the generating stations into its path?"

"Impossible," Chang said slowly. "It would take months."

"The drive units are still orbiting around Terra," Mendoza said. "Can we interpose one of the stations?"

"As a last resort . . . perhaps. But that knocks the Artery out of business for a year."

"We can't have that," Mendoza said. "We can't survive even six more months without the Artery's fissionable."

"What if we don't stop the beam?" Beckworth asked.

"If just the fringes of the atmosphere are involved," Bayerd said, "the beam will lose only a fraction of its kinetic energy. There'll be heat generated but not so much that it won't be dissipated without danger."

"And if it penetrates more deeply?" Gilchrist asked.

"A great deal more heat, secondary radiation from the high speed of the beam, ionization, shock waves from the localized heating."

"And what does that mean in terms of damage?" Gilchrist demanded.

"I'm afraid," Adrianne said slowly, "that it might mean a great deal. The radiation can probably be discounted. Mostly short half-lives. The shock wave could be disastrous. The effect of so much heat generated in the path of the beam would be equivalent to a giant meteor penetrating the atmosphere."

"Chang," Bayerd said, "what's the situation at the capsule?"

"This is not easy," Chang said slowly. "We have lowered four robot units to the bottom of the shaft and are sending down cutting tools."

"Any chance of blasting?"

"Through the metal? I do not think it advisable."

"Give me an estimate of how quickly you can get to the capsule."

"That I will have in another hour."

"My God," Bayerd said, "an hour? We've got only sixteen before that damned thing is keyed to start spraying plasma all over the system."

"This had to happen," Gilchrist said. "You can't

stake the whole future of a world on a gamble like this."

"Councilman," Bayerd said, "Terra won't have a future if we start to panic."

"You forget yourself," Gilchrist said, jumping to his feet. Mendoza half-rose, trying to restrain him.

Gilchrist seemed to swell for an instant in his fury. Then he turned without speaking and stalked from the room. Mendoza said, "Damn it, Norm, watch your temper. You can do both of us a lot of harm," and followed Gilchrist from the room.

"You know how most of the commercial space drives operate?" Bayerd asked Adrianne.

"A combination chemical plasma system?"

"That's right. They throw colloidal aluminum into an arc chamber to increase the arc temperature by a magnetoconstriction effect, accelerate the metal vapor jet to supersonic by an eddy-current funnel, and then get the last bit of juice out of the fuel by injecting water to oxidize the aluminum. The point is that they throw out a wake of colloidal aluminum oxide, and each particle is charged. What would happen if the beam penetrated a large enough cross section of that stuff?"

"Something as tenuous as that?" she said. "It can't possibly stop the beam."

"Not stop," Bayerd said. "Just deflect. Each one of those colloidal particles of aluminum oxide is charged. How large a cross section do we need to deflect each individual plasmoid of the beam just the bit necessary to make sure it misses Terra?"

"I can run it on the Station computer with sure feedback from Pelambang," she said, moving toward the hatch. "It might work."

"That leaves me pretty much dead weight," Beckworth said when only he, McDow, and Bayerd were left on the bridge.

"How's your supply of pep pills?"

"Stimulants. Well, I've a fair supply of PALA, para-amino-lacto-amphetamine, but I don't like to use the stuff except in an emergency."

"This is an emergency in spades," Bayerd said. "Look, we're going to have to keep driving these men for the next sixteen hours at least, probably longer. They'll be dead for sleep, and we need everyone. At top alertness, top efficiency."

"All right," Beckworth said, "but you'd better radio for replacements. I want those men off their feet and in bed for at least forty-eight hours afterward."

He paused, looked expectantly at Bayerd, then said, "And I won't give over a hundred fifty milligrams to any man, regardless of what you say."

Bayerd turned to McDow.

"Then give the situation down below. I want a complete new crew up here in twenty-four hours, with another standing by Earthside. And press them to get us that ship data. I want cargoes as well."

"Cargoes?" McDow asked.

Bayerd pressed his hand over his head and sighed tiredly. "Playing to a blind hand. Still, you never know what one might be carrying that would prove useful."

"Right," McDow said and started for the hatch.

As soon as he was out of earshot, Beckworth said, "All right, Norm, sit down a minute."

"Haven't got time."

"You'll take time. I want to take a look at you."

"There's nothing wrong with me," Bayerd said.

"That's for me to say," Beckworth said, pushing him into a chair. He felt for Bayerd's pulse, paused as he checked the count, and then produced a small pencil light from his pocket. After a moment looking at each eye and pursing his lips, he said, "What are you taking?"

"Nothing."

"Don't give me that."

Bayerd started, then tried to speak. Finally he nothing.

"Tranquilizer?" Beckworth asked.

Bayered started, then tried to speak. Finally he nodded.

"What for?" Beckworth demanded.

"I've been a little jumpy lately," Bayerd said. "Nothing serious." He patted the vial of capsules in his breast pocket.

"I think you should be in bec'," Beckworth said. "You look like a man who's gone through a concrete mixer."

"Don't talk to me about resting at a time like this," Bayerd said impatiently. "I can't even think in those terms for the next twenty-four hours."

"All right, all right," Beckworth said. "Kill yourself. That's your privilege, but watch your step each minute. Those things, coupled with fatigue, can affect your judgment, your reaction time. And I want a detailed physical on you as soon as this mess is cleared up."

Bayerd shifted his weight uncomfortably in the chair, feeling like a small boy who has been caught stealing cookies.

"I'll have it done my next Earthside trip," he said.

"Huh uh," Beckworth objected. "That's my department. I want an official record on anyone connected with the project. I haven't received one for you from below, and I want to run a few tests."

"Don't be so damned persistent," Bayerd said tiredly.

"That's what I get paid for," the medic said.

While van der Reis slept his brief nap, the news filtered through the computer station. At first no one fully understood the significance of the mistake on far Pluto. Martin was dimly aware of the undercurrent of worry that filtered through the ranks of the technicians, but he was far too concerned with his own immediate project to realize, as the final computations developed, that the first traces of panic might be developing within the computer cadre.

The news of any disaster has a perverse, almost masochistic effect on human beings. Historically, all impending disasters have been exaggerated in the telling from mouth to mouth. It's a human and natural thing to thrill to the feeling of impending danger, the feeling of personal disaster hanging above one's head by the merest thread. The Damoclean Sword has a particularly perverse appeal to human beings. The quiet conviction of personal immortality probably assures every human that nothing really terrible and final can happen to him. Yet in the latter days of the human race, more and more instances had arisen to threaten the basic existence of the race until any new danger triggered a particularly self-punishing thrill among human society.

By the time the course of the rumor had run through the Pelambang Station, the night news crew around the island was already alerted and dispatching teams to the station, while others were already radioing Europe, where the master coordinating centers of the Artery were located, and New York, where the Power Allotment Board was in continuous twenty-four-hour meeting, attempting to resolve the delicate anomalies of the Liechtenstein census.

Carmelita had rested for several hours now, and much against the advice of the local physician, was up and reporting for duty. Her initial reaction to the news was one of horror. She had been accustomed to working through the local Shrenk units on the Artery itself, managing several of the local data-gathering units, and she had perhaps a better view of the awful power of the Plutonian installation than many of the other members of the Pelambang staff.

When the first inquiries from Adrianne Patel came to her station, she thought that there must be something indeed wrong with the data. Seconds later the full import of the emergency hit her, and she called Martin.

"I know," he said. "Karl briefed me earlier. I'm sorry I can't help you, but he's given me another assignment."

"It's easy enough to see why you don't want to help," she said, feeling miffed.

"Oh, for God's sake," he snapped. "You know better than that."

"I've seen you mooning around him lately," she snapped. "You know that's against the contract."

"Why don't you take that up with Karl," he snapped. "I've been very concerned about you, but I'm not going to cater to your female suspicions."

"You little tin . . ." she began and snapped the connection before she finished the invective. The word "bastard" lingered in her mind. She was quite sure that it was a piece of invective that would not have occurred to Martin.

She thought of calling van der Reis, but she decided that he needed the bit of precious rest he was taking and that she might best continue on the calculations. In the meantime she knew that other data were coming in on the placement of several other craft of diverse characteristics throughout the system. There was a massive effort on to intercept this section of beam, and she could well see why. If indeed the beam did intersect the Earth-moon system, particularly if it did impinge on the Earth's atmosphere, the results would be disastrous. She shuddered at the thought.

In his cubicle van der Reis stirred fitfully, already half awake. His usual talent for quick catnaps that stood him in such good stead during this long duty session had failed him. He felt severely troubled on several levels. He had been disturbed for some time over the apparent dissolution of the close emotional ties in his metafamily, particularly with the developing emotional incompatibilities of Martin and Carmelita. Had he been asked for a decision as to which was his favorite, he would have been hard pressed. It was regrettable. They had worked so well together for so long. Now, overlaying this concern was the pressing worry of the new emergency and the vague realization that there was more than a casual interest in Martin's work on Bayerd's model. He felt the distinct nagging intuition that here too a secret and dark danger was developing.

It was in this half-drowsy disoriented mood that he stared into the darkness of the cubicle, his eyes suddenly open and probing as though into a distance far beyond the close-clinging walls. What had brought him to this alertness?

For a moment he could not answer the question. Then he realized that it was the vague feeling, almost intuition of another presence, another intelligence within the room. Well, not within the room but within thought distance. A faint chill touched his skin. He stared into the blackness, vainly seeking.

In the next instant he was looking down long unending distances. It was the most acute kind of tunnel vision, straining his eyes with the impossible adjustments that the muscles must make. He saw distant vistas of waving grasses and swirling splotches of fire-veined darkness, moving masses that resolved themselves into people . . . the swirling mass that became a man . . . the man, he realized, who had accosted him in the nether part of the station.

He felt as if the very substance of his body were being sucked out of him. In the next instant he was falling dizzily into a gelatinous blackness, feeling his very self enveloped in cloying, suffocating folds. In the last instant he cried out.

Carmelita had, almost as a matter of course, been monitoring his room, waiting for some change in his breathing rate that would tell her he was awake. It was not the invasion of privacy that a single might have thought it, but rather the normal practice of one concerned member of a metafamily to another.

When van der Reis screamed, she reacted immediately. Her finger touched the hold plate of the programmer, and she was out of her seat in a second. She ran down the corridor and pushed into the blackened cubicle. She whistled the low note that keyed the lights.

He was lying on the couch, his eyes wide and unfocused, looking into impossible distances. Even as she watched, the bright color of his tunic faded to a neutral shade, his eyes lost their features, his face became a mere sketch of brow and nose and mouth.

She must have gasped in that moment. He looked at her in terror and then simply . . . ceased to be.

Bayerd guided his chair from the bridge and returned to the "S" deck where he felt more comfortable. He was about to pull himself from his prosthetic chair and enter his Shrenk capsule when Mendoza appeared in the hatch and said, "Norm, may I speak with you?"

"I'm tired of talking," Bayerd said irritably. "It seems that this is all we have time for. There's a great deal to do now."

"This is important," Mendoza said. "I've got to know for my own purposes. What are the chances of intercepting the beam?"

"I don't know," Bayerd said tiredly. "I wish I could give you an answer, but I don't really know any more than I told you all at the briefing. We assume that we have a good reading on the transmission, but there are uncertainties in that and in the later calculations of its path. We assume that the techniques we discussed for intercepting or deflecting the beam will work, but all of this is theory. We can only try and hope."

Mendoza snorted impatiently. "It's not as simple as that," he said. "I can't tell my opponents back on Earth that they must simply wait and trust. This whole situation would conceivably give the Eastern Combine the lever they need for a bigger power ration. Up to now the ration has been the basis of pre-Artery power usage modified by population growth. Africa and Asia have always had bigger birth rates, and we've had to do quite a bit of juggling to keep the present level of Western technology properly supplied with power resources."

Bayerd rubbed his chin wearily. "I don't see how this ties in with the present situation."

"Well," Mendoza paused for a second, then seemed to come to a decision, "you may as well know. All hell will break loose at the next session. We forced this Liechtenstein scandal. Accused them of falsifying the census records to up their power allotment. It was easy to do. Small district and not too many people to get to. The idea was to throw doubt on the larger census areas."

"I can well see why you have a crisis on your hands. The ways of politicians never cease to amaze me," Bayerd paused. "I wish," he said slowly, "that you hadn't told me of this."

"Politics is always dirty when national survival is at stake," Mendoza said. "Don't you see that the West . . . Amazonia, the American States . . . are the best hope of solving the basic mess we're in. We're the technological leaders, the countries needing the most power . . ."

"I'm sorry," Bayerd said, shaking his head. "I appreciate all you've done for the project, but I don't want to be a party to anything like this, regardless of what you want from me."

"Damn it, Norm, I'm not asking you to be a party to anything. I'm trying to be honest with you so you'll understand why you can't allow Gilchrist to involve you in any personal issues. Shifting attention from an issue to a personality conflict is the oldest trick in the book. Don't give him the chance."

Bayerd thought for a moment and then eyed the councilman. Mendoza's olive face was shining with perspiration, and his black eyes dropped to the floor when Bayerd looked at him.

"Oh, I know, damn it," Mendoza said. "I get a little sick of the mess myself sometimes. I fight for what I believe in, Norm, just as you do. And dirty if I have to. We're alike in that respect."

Bayerd ignored the thrust and said, "Look, just how dirty will their side fight?"

"Hard to say; what's on your mind?"

Bayerd told him about the changed settings on the capsule.

"My good Lord," Mendoza said. "Whoever would do such a thing? He must be insane."

"Not necessarily," Bayerd said. "He could have intended the beam to go out into space. The chances were all in favor of that."

"But the capsule . . ."

"Someone wants the beam shut down for a time. What he didn't anticipate was that the mechanisms in the capsule would continue to transmit the beam and that we would not be able to get to the capsule in time."

"What are our chances there?"

"That's what I'm trying to find out," Bayerd said, gesturing toward the Shrenk cubicles. "I want to check on the spot and see how Chang's crew is coming."

"Is it possible at all to get to the accelerator?"

"The magnetic fields would disrupt robot control."

"Can't you just cut off the ore supply to the smelters?"

"We've done that," Bayerd said, "but there's about a ten-minute reserve within the accelerator area."

Mendoza sighed. "Then if you have not cut down to the capsule in the next fifteen hours, you must stop transmission some other way."

"No one's touching that installation," Bayerd said angrily.

"What do you want?" Mendoza said. "Do you want your equipment intact and that uncontrolled beam running through the system? You said there's enough reserve metal within the system for four days of transmission, and what may not happen in that time?"

"You can't touch the accelerator," Bayerd said angrily.

"When the time comes, if you can't give the order . . ." Mendoza said and then didn't finish the statement.

Bayerd stared at him, and the full import of what he was saying slowly dawned on him. He felt his whole body suddenly quiver with rage. "Is it that easy?" he demanded. "You're willing to destroy the Artery, the work of a lifetime, and the only hope of maintaining this precarious technology we've been building over the century."

"Yes," Mendoza said tiredly. "Yes, if the alternative is the possibility of more complete destruction, particularly if the alternative is what we now think it may be."

"You can all go to hell," Bayerd said and hit the controls of the chair with his right hand. The chair twisted rapidly, off balance for a moment and then the automatic gyros righted it, their quick precision partially countering the side impulse.

"Norm," Mendoza called, but Bayerd ignored him. His rage was too complete, too consuming to differentiate between friend and foe. He knew only that he wanted to get away from the man, from all the simpering, maneuvering men who did not understand the soul and nature of this thing he had created.

He guided his chair into the Shrenk cubicle and heard the door iris behind him. He leaned back, feeling the mangaluminum solidarity of the chair through the cloth of his tunic and behind him the almost womblike security of the Shrenk cubicle wall, the irised door closing him off from the menace of Mendoza and the others. He felt emotionally drained, as though he had been laughing or crying for hours. A part of him still churned with rage at Mendoza's sudden betrayal.

He pulled himself from the chair with the overhead bar and seated himself on the webbing of the Shrenk suit, buckling the mesh about his weakened legs. The chest harness felt cold and constricting as he moved the facepiece toward him.

He felt the tension stealing over him, the quivering of thighs and the tightness of jaw muscles. If he could just hold off until the mess was finished. He freed his hand and fumbled for the medicine in his pocket, thinking of how they symbolized the thin distance between him and the end, not only of his personal existence, but in a larger sense the end of the existence of this entity he had created out of his life and his brain and his body.

He thrust his left arm into the glove, activating the controls for the robot atop the lookout point and thrust his bead into the facepiece. The image of the two cathode tubes reflected in the angled immors of the facepiece lightened for a second, flared, and . . .

And he was looking out over the deserted rock, seeing the dead control consoles, the empty robot bodies standing apart where they had been thoughtlessly abandoned. He made walking motions in the harness and moved to the console he had occupied just before the transmission. He activated the metering circuits and checked the board. One meter registering grid potentials on the self-contained amplifier flickered, but the rest were dead. He touched the remote-register and a dim picture flickered on the tube, transmitted from the face of the capsule, buried in the rock. He saw the loose locking screws and the fatal setting on the face of the capsule. There could be no doubt about it. The settings were quite different than the ones he had placed on the capsule the day before. He tried to think back. Could he have possibly made a mistake, changed one of the settings while he was adjusting the automatic timing device? No, to make such an error he would have to have changed three settings from those the Earthside computers at Pelambang had given them. The change was deliberate. No doubt of it.

Then the thought hit him. Whoever had changed the settings might conceivably have trapped himself without knowing it. He stooped and slid back the panel in the base of the console. Inside, a series of coils of tape recorded the reading of the meters above from moment to moment. Normally they were erased after every twenty-four hours unless they were needed to compute some slight adjustment of the beam inherently undetectable by the beam's own mechanisms.

He extracted the two tapes that recorded deflection and elevation of the transmitted beam and laid them on the surface of the console. After a moment of searching, he found the spot on one where the capsule setting had been changed and then he found the similar change on the other spool. He noted the time on each and rewound the tapes. Then he found a small wrench in a nearby kit and carefully unseated the oscilloscope from the upper right-hand corner of the console panel. He wedged the two spools into the space beside the tapering tube and reseated it. Then he threaded two new spools onto the recording devices. Now, he thought, should anyone else have the same idea, they would think that the spools had been erased.

Then he rose and walked to the edge of the precipice. Below he could see the capsule installation, its ceramic shield peeled away like the husk of a walnut. There were two Shrenk robots on the near side, struggling with a heavy mass that he finally identified as a generator for a monatomic hydrogen cutting torch.

"This is Bayerd," he said. "How much progress are you making?"

"Trubner here," the voice came back. "The other generator broke down. We had to bring this one up from the mining installations."

"Hold it a minute," Bayerd said. He withdrew from the facepiece, and for a moment the confusion of the transition startled him. He touched the switch that activated the robot unit on the plain, and suddenly as he returned to the facepiece he was standing a hundred yards from the group with the generator. He walked over and said,

"Here, I'll handle the rear."

"Thanks," said a voice that he identified as Muletti's. He had a mental image of the small, wiry Italian, his normally curly black hair clipped short in the matted crewcut. Carefully he moved the generator toward the capsule shield and then slowly set it on the rock.

"I'll get it hooked up," Muletti volunteered.

"Good," Bayerd said, turning to look out over the plain. The accelerator installations still glowed with the bright radiance of infrared near the smelters. The scene reminded him of something out of a surrealist painting with the inverted highlights seemingly twisting the familiar shapes into alien forms. Strange to think that this great thing of metals and energies might soon end.

It would be so easy, though, he thought. There were three cargo ships based to the south near the ore pits. One need only man a ship, take it up, and crash-dive it into the installation. No necessity of using explosives. Only . . .

That would be killing the Artery. And the man piloting the ship would die a kind of death, though vicariously.

If it had to be done, he promised himself, it would be done at his hand. He would ride the ship down, die flaming in the wreck, and walk the Black Field Station afterward to die another kind of death.

Then he thought of why he had come. "Trubner," he said, "switch to the 'A' net."

When Trubner responded over the new channel, Bayerd said, "How soon after I gave the order did you seat the capsule?"

"Three . . . four minutes, I suppose."

"Did you log it on your tape?"

"Yes," Trubner said.

"Check it, will you?"

Trubner's robot became immobile. Bayerd waited impatiently for seconds, then turned to watch Muletti lowering the generator through the shielding into the capsule pit. They had improvised a second winch to replace the one damaged by the arcing, welding the drum to the interior metal frame of the shield.

"Who's down below?" Bayerd asked.

"Sanchez, Chang, and Girard," Muletti said.

"How are they coming?"

"Very hard working. The metal spattered, however, so that it's somewhat porous, and we occasionally cut into a series of vapor pockets, which helps."

"Good," Bayerd said, as Trubner's body came erect.

"The time was 9:02," Trubner said.

"Are you sure? I have to have this pinpointed."

"Yes. I was recording from the command net. I dictated the time as I started to lower the capsule. It checks with the time index on the tape."

"That would mean about 9:01 for your time of arrival at the capsule site itself."

"I should think so."

"Thanks," Bayerd said. As Trubner returned to work, he deactivated the body and he was again in the station, leaning tiredly into the Shrenk harness. He freed himself and debated his next move. The obvious one was to check the tapes on each Shrenk unit. Find the one showing a break in control a minute or so before 9:01, Pelambang time.

Overhead an intercom speaker crackled and McDow's voice said, "Norm, can you come up to Commo? I've got your shipping information."

He made his way up to Commo to find McDow and Patel seated at the transceiver. McDow sprang to his feet and held out a pad. "There's the story," he said.

Bayerd scanned the sheet, noting orbital figures, velocities, and said, "Never mind. You've screened these already. What can we use?"

"Here," McDow said, "we've made a sketch." He unfolded a sheet of five-foot-square graph paper and fastened the sheet to the bulkhead with gummed tape. He had sketched in the orbits of the Earth and the planets past her out to Pluto. The distances were not to scale, Bayerd saw, the transjovian distances being much foreshortened. Beside each orbital circle he had noted figures in hours and minutes, denoting, Bayerd decided, the anticipated progress of the beam front.

"This is all approximate," McDow said. "You'll notice that Terra is 'zero' and 'Pluto' is twenty hours. The beam front is approximately at this point." He touched a spot just outside of the orbit of Uranus and made a small "x" with his pencil, labeling it "10 Hours."

"All right," Bayerd said, "give me the ships."

"Six of various size including the *Ingrid*, a cruiser assigned to the Norwegian Astronomical Society, and a Karmanship, the *SAU-62*, carrying air to the Callisto Experimental Ecological Station. All in this general sector." He pointed at the area past Jupiter and near Saturn. At this point he penciled the inscription: "Approx. 4 Hours."

"Then," he said, consulting the sheet, "there's an ion-drive freighter, the *CX-248*, here just above the asteroid belt. Cargo is an orbital radar lens for the radio telescope the Council is building in the Trojans, you know, one of those big inflatable polyparalene balloons plated with a layer of sodium metal. There are also four other plasma-drive ships and one chemical ballistic freighter in the same region. It's only an hour and forty minutes to 'zero' at that point though."

Bayerd looked at the sketch. The Karmanship, the *SAU*-62, near Saturn, might be promising. Karmanships were huge cargo vessels operating on a hothouse principle, trapping solar energy in a sphere of thin plastic and using the energy to heat hydrogen for expulsion. They were capable of an acceleration of perhaps one-thousandth of a gravity. The trip to Saturn, if he recalled correctly, took almost nine months with a hundred thirty days or so of acceleration and an equal period for deceleration. That meant that the drifter was barely moving at this point so close to its destination.

He checked the sheet for the data on the second drifter above the asteroid belt. The ship, he saw, had been out of Terra orbit sixty-seven days and now had a velocity of two hundred miles per hour. That was not exceptionally high, he realized, but the fragile construction of the vessels, which were never meant to withstand a strong acceleration, made maneuvering the things a touchy proposition.

"Adrianne," Bayerd asked, "what about the exhaust trick?"

"I ran the calculations on it," she said. "The theory is pretty, of course. You can build up quite a few statcoulombs on the particle cloud but they're moving pretty fast at that temperature and the particles are all charged alike, which means they repel each other. A ten-mile cross section might give you the three-tenths of a second deflection you need at Saturn's orbit, but you couldn't hold the cloud together even if you had the fuel for the density I calculated. No good, I'm afraid."

"It was a wild idea, anyway," Bayerd said.

"If we can set up an electrostatic point source close enough to the beam path, we might deflect it," she said. "It would deform the plasmoids, but the later impulse might be sufficient to deflect the beam enough."

"All right," Bayerd said, "we'll play both cards out. Let's see if we can move the *SAU-62* into the beam path with the ships in the area and build up a skin charge using the motors of the other ships. We can cut out the charge dissipators and throw out every bit of mass. That should build up a pretty good charge."

"What about the freighter in the asteroid belt?"

"The *CX-248*? We'll do the same with it. We'll have to have close observations of the path of the beam. Can that Norwegian ship give it to us?"

"Wait," Adrianne said. "Norm, what about the freighter with the radar lens? Can't we unship it and inflate it in space? With so much of a metallic surface, we could accumulate an enormous charge."

"It won't work," McDow said.

"We've got to give it a try," Bayerd snapped.

"That's not what I mean. Ion-drive freighters are fairly fragile. They're not intended for high accelerations. The *CX-248* might take one 'g' but not much more without breaking up. At one-'g' deceleration, it will take about ten hours to decelerate the *CX-248*, and we simply don't have that long."

Bayerd rubbed his hand tiredly across his eyes and said, "Then we'll just have to do without it."

"No, of course not," Adrianne said. "It's the polyparalene lens we want. We can decelerate the ship even if it does buckle. Just so long as our lens is intact."

"Of course," Bayerd said. Then: "How much time does the first group have?"

"About six hours," McDow responded. "Roughly eight and a half for the second group."

Bayerd directed his chair past the two and said to McDow, "Better raise Luna Station and give me a line to the president of the Council. We'll need his weight behind us before we can start tearing up somebody else's property."

As McDow called Luna Station, Bayerd was thinking of what he had discovered at the accelerator site. Then he remembered the conversation with Muletti. He had, he realized, forgotten to change back to the command net after talking with Trubner. Yet Muletti had answered him immediately when he spoke.

Why, Bayerd wondered, had the man been eavesdropping on his conversation with Trubner?

He cut from the Shrenk robot and found himself again in the cubicle on the Black Field Station. He thought of the silent world turning far below and the sleeping millions, as yet unaware of the fiery disaster arrowing toward them at a quarter of the speed of light. No, he thought, not unaware, for by now the news must surely be out, and the various local governments must be organizing their information services to prevent the developing panic.

"Norman," McDow's voice said near his ear. He touched the plate on the console before him, and the man's face appeared in the small viewscreen.

"Yes," he said.

"There's something very strange coming in from

Pelambang," McDow said. "I don't know quite what to make of it. You recall van der Reis's girl, Carmelita O'Fallon?"

Bayerd said that he did.

"She's just returned from Luzon where she apparently ran into a rather unsettling thing . . . something to do with the sort of temporal phenomena we've been experiencing lately. Anyway, she's been in the Pelambang Station hospital since she returned."

"Was she injured?" Bayerd asked.

"No, apparently shaken up. She was supposed to return to duty later this evening. You know we're pretty short-handed down there. Anyway, she's one of van der Reis's metafamily and . . ."

Bayerd snorted in spite of himself. "Ah, yes, those damned cultists and their new familial structures."

"Well, there's a strong emotional bond that grows up in such a situation," McDow protested. "She sensed something was wrong with van der Reis and left the dispensary to find him. She had just entered his sleep room when it happened."

"Stop being so mysterious," Bayerd said irritably. "What happened?"

"I'm still not sure," McDow said. "She says that he disappeared."

"Disappeared?"

"That's right," McDow said tiredly. "She says he just seemed to flicker in and out of focus and then he . . . well, she says he just evaporated. Does that make sense?"

Bayerd thought tiredly, Sense? What makes sense any more? At last he said, "Yes, it does make a kind of sense. How it fits in I'm not sure, but it does make a kind of horrible sense."

Chapter Seven

H PLUS NINE HOURS

The thousand-meter segment of the Artery is well inside the orbit of Uranus now, traveling at slightly over a quarter of the speed of light. It crossed the orbit of Uranus approximately one hour before, intersecting that invisible line at slightly over 1.7 billion miles from the sun. Against this distance the mere 93 million miles that separate the Earth and the sun are trivial.

The segment is a faint broken line of blue against the star-punctuated black of space. It is already beginning to show an infinitesimal curvature as the faint radiant energy of the sun pushes against it. The individual plasmoids have broadened ever so slightly, but the beam is maintaining its integrity well. At this speed relativistic effects are such that the mass of the individual plasmoids has increased approximately 3 percent. The total kinetic energy of the beam, however, is enormous. Its collision with a surface would instantly at this point yield something on the order of 10^{15} kilogram-calories, a formidable amount of energy to be concentrated in a relatively narrow cross section.

The invisible area on Earth has expanded inexorably, its lateral borders proceeding at a varying pace. There is a distinct area in which the effects oscillated as though some secondary planetary wobble has introduced a pulse to the intersection. The line of influence in the Orient has extended now across the Russian steppes, curving downward through the western edge of Sinkiang, vertically bisecting India and curving eastward again through the Indian Ocean. The effects in India are hardly noticed, for that steaming, crowded land has continued its slow, inevitable slide back through time. India was lost in the latter part of the twentieth century, and not even the level of technology supported by the new power sources of the Artery do more than yield a subsistence living for its billions. Even if a successful breeder pile technology had been developed in the late eighties, the inevitable trend could not have been reversed. The subcontinent is quite accustomed to mystics and to inexplicable departures from the pedestrian pragmatism of the times. The sudden appearances of long-dead pavans of bejeweled and silk-clad princes in the streets of Bombay are the cause of scarcely a glance. The princes themselves do not trouble their eyes with the stinking streets outside their gauze-festooned sedans. To them twenty-first-century India looks very much like sixteenth-century India. They are only vaguely curious about transmission towers and clumsy self-powered vehicles that thread the streets. To be otherwise is to behave vulgarly.

To the east of Pelambang, the line of influence is approaching Hawaii. The pattern of human migration through the ages has crossed and crossed this zone again. In a sweeping cross section of millions of years of human history, however, the chances of the zone intersecting specific bands of roaming humans is statistically much lower than in the crowded continent of

Asia. Still, a floating deep-sea processing station does report sighting a distant group of outriggers of the type that had not been seen in the area for six decades. A passing hovercraft attempts to hail them without success and returns to base with its fuselage studded with six-inch darts that appear to have been designed for some kind of simple sling.

The alarm that had started shortly after 9:00 P.M. Pelambang time, when the Artery pulse was transmitted, had now spread throughout the station. The early rumors that leaked to the press hit the satellite services some three hours later. Various technicians at the computer complex found their exits blocked in the period as Means, acting with characteristic bluntness, declared a general security block at the station. This was all that was necessary to confirm what the news services had already suspected, that something was amiss at the station, or worse, with the Artery. The news services in the area were controlled by H plus ten, but the damage had been done. Much of the speculation prior to this time had been surprisingly accurate, although no single newsman had truly perceived the actual magnitude of the accident that now hurled a thousand meters of ionized metallic plasmoids sunward at one-quarter the speed of light.

For Carmelita the second encounter with the unpredictable influence spreading across the Pacific areas and the Asian continent had resulted not in hysteria, but in a kind of dull shock. Martin was the first to reach her after she had sounded the alarm, and his quiet concern did more than anything to cushion the shock. When she was finally able to speak, she detailed what she had observed in a quiet, dispassionate voice.

In the two hours following van der Reis's disappearance, she moved into her normal position of third to van der Reis, displacing a confused Means to a more pedestrian administrative job.

"I think," she told Martin, "that you should take over the station operation."

"Under ordinary circumstances, I would," he assured her. "Karl thought that the model should have priority, and I am more and more inclined to believe him. Besides, you can handle the job."

She seemed lost in thought. "I don't know," she said. "The first order of business is to activate the new cells."

"Can we safely do that without damaging them permanently?" he asked.

"I don't know," she said, "but we must chance it. Fenrenc in New York thinks so. They've all been checked out rather thoroughly in the past four weeks. We must have the extra capacity for the next few hours."

"We've integrated them into the total information complex only in sections," he reminded her.

"I know," she said tiredly. "Do you think we're taking too great a chance?"

"I don't see that we have any choice," he told her. His voice was soft and concerned. Her tightly controlled expression wavered and seemed to dissolve for an instant in fear before her control reasserted itself.

"Take it easy," he told her quietly. "You'll do fine."

"What could have happened?" she said quietly. "First the Artery transmission, now Karl."

"There is," Martin said thoughtfully, quite unaware of her light touch on his shoulder, "an interconnection of events, no question of that." He laughed bitterly. "An almost mystical interconnection, one might even say."

"I can almost accept the word," she replied. "Certainly it seems a possible one after the way Karl . . ." She shuddered and did not finish the sentence.

"This damnable business of waiting," McDow said, his voice husky with fatigue. "You feel so completely helpless."

"There's nothing we can do but wait," Bayerd said.

"You look very tired, Norm," McDow said, his voice suddenly solicitous. "Why don't you get some sleep. I'll wake you if anything comes in."

Bayerd shook his head slowly. "I've reached a point where I can't sleep over four hours," he said. "I'd just as soon be up and about. Besides, I'd like to check with Chang's group at the transmitter. God, they've got to get through to that thing before too many hours." He maneuvered his chair toward the hatch, then stopped. "I know I'm sounding a little paranoid," he said, "but do me a favor. Keep your eye on Gilchrist and Adrianne, will you?"

"Do you think it's either of them?" McDow said. "No, that wouldn't make any sense at all, particularly the woman. She would never dream of taking such an overt action."

"Perhaps," Bayerd said. "The whole business is completely insane. I don't know whom to trust at this point, but it's clear that someone intimately involved with the operation of the past ten hours is responsible for what happened."

All the way down to the Shrenk cubicles, Bayerd could feel the growing tenseness of his body. His wasted muscles were carrying fatigue he had not felt in years. He realized that he had never been filled with such a dread before. The terrible burden of responsibility of the Artery was weight enough, but the consequences of the emergency now facing him haunted his mind. He knew that he should rest, that the buildup of fatigue might easily precipitate an attack at the time when he could least afford it.

"Take it easy," the doctors had told him. "Don't fatigue yourself, keep up the medication, and there's no reason why, under zero 'g,' that you shouldn't lead a long and full life."

Full life, he thought bitterly. To be confined bodily to this station with only the surrogate release of that other body, to be an observer of humanity but not a participant in it. To watch the slow deterioration of one's body and watch each tiny symptom. It was like carrying death as a sable shadow on the rim of your consciousness for the rest of your years. He had read extensively about his illness, but he knew little more than when he had started. There were, of course, completely atypical symptoms that he had ascribed to the prolonged effect of weightlessness. After some initial periods of decalcification during the first year, he had reached a metabolic steady state. The occasional disorientations as that one terrible loss of consciousness years before still frightened him. The doctors had explained it rather simply as a sudden drop in blood glucose, a momentary hypoglycemia, but he had been very careful after that to make sure that he did not override his declining endurance.

He thought of McDow's advice, but he knew that he could not rest now, not with his mind heaving restlessly and the fear nibbling at the edge of his consciousness. He could not rest as long as the man who had tampered with the Artery was free and undiscovered. (Man? Why necessarily a man? It could easily have been her. No, he could not accept that. There were too many memories of tenderness and things shared before that last climactic confrontation.) Who was it, then? Chang? Trubner? Muletti? One of their crew? Or McDow? No, he couldn't believe that. McDow was devoted to the project. It was more than a job to him. Why, he remembered when McDow had been first assigned to his staff.

When McDow had joined the beam project fifteen years before, Bayerd had said, "Operating the Artery will be like standing back a hundred yards and stoking a furnace by throwing capped blocks of TNT at the open door. As long as your aim is good, the TNT lands inside and burns quietly. But if you miss, chances are the block will land on its fulminate cap. That won't do a great deal of damage, but suppose the furnace supplies the only heat there is in one of the polar cities and suppose there's a tank of chlorine stored in the same room. Now, if you miss the door and the TNT explodes, the tank goes up too and you poison the whole block, perhaps the whole city. But you've got to keep the fire going or the whole city freezes."

"So," McDow had said, "you keep the game going because the city can't survive otherwise, and you pray your aim is good."

"Which is why you're part of the project," Bayerd said.

"Because I'm to be trusted with TNT?"

"Because," Bayerd said, "we think your aim is good."

And so far, Bayerd thought, so far their aim had

been good. When they first built the Artery, he had held doubts, secret doubts that he would never have admitted. How could you concede a possibility to an antagonist without his seizing it, emphasizing it in terms of black and white, beating it out of shape with endless argument until a possibility became a probability and then a certainty? That's what would have happened with the Artery had he agreed that the possibility of misdirection, of loss of control, existed.

When he had first conceived of the project, she had been beside him, helping him with the most difficult parts of the calculations, ever ready with some special bit of knowledge that he did not have. He had come to her with the idea after the discovery of the great beds of uranium hydride on Pluto and she had agreed that, with the failure of breeder pile technology to provide the needed fissionables for Earth, this seemed the surest approach to solving the power famine. They had been well advanced into the project before she began to have her doubts. Her calculations during that period showed that it would be increasingly difficult to control the Artery as Pluto moved to aphelion. He insisted that newer technology would solve the problem before they had to face it.

Concurrent with her work on the Artery, she looked more deeply into the years of fruitless work to develop a controlled fusion process. The one area that increasingly engaged her attention was not the magnetohydrodynamic research of half a century, but the approach that involved achieving fusion temperatures in a deuterium-tritium container without use of a magnetic bottle to contain the intensely hot plasma. The approach in this case was to use a high-energy laser pulse that produced the needed temperatures in tiny fractions of a second and depend on the sheer inertia of the gases to contain the fusion spot. Not even the first disastrous explosion that leveled the British experimental station on the Isle of Man in the first instant of operation, vaporizing tons of rock and dirt and scattering radioactive ash abroad on the winds, had discouraged her. By this time she was convinced that this was the way to go. Since the amount of money available could not support both the extensive fusion research and the incredible feat of building the Artery, what had started as a disagreement, and later a gentle rivalry, became a full-scale political confrontation.

Peculiarly enough, both arguments hinged on the Black Field effect, that strange accidental by-product of binding energy research that promised up to 20 percent conversion of matter in the fission reaction by its ability to contain the incredible forces of even an atomic explosion. Actually, "contain" wasn't the proper term. The Black Field partitioned energy within its influence in a most complex fashion. Particles with a given kinetic energy within the field crossed its boundaries and emerged with that energy much reduced. This was controllable. The density of the field would yield reductions of energy of from 80 to almost 100 percent. Coincidently, a certain number of particles in any group disappeared utterly. Statistically, the mass loss could be related to the reciprocal of the energy loss. The effect was essentially linear.

A German physicist named Kulz found that reversing the polarity of the field under certain conditions resulted in a failure to contain the energy of the nuclear reaction. Had he not communicated his intended experiment to a colleague in Pakistan, no one would have known what happened. One thing developed from the disastrous experiment. Even if you calculated the energy release from total conversion of the contained mass, you came out with less energy than actually released. Something for nothing. Energy out of nowhere. Perpetual motion.

Only it wasn't so.

A team financed by the World Council finally came up with a theory that seemed to fit the facts. There was . . . incredibly . . . complete conversion within the normally operating field, or very nearly complete conversion of mass into energy. Not just binding energy, the inconsequential residue of splitting into simpler atoms, but complete annihilation of matter. The initial stage was simple fission, but the Black Field's energy-partitioning effect came into operation. A small portion of the enclosed matter gained the major portion of energy within the field and achieved velocities exceeding that of light in fractions of a microsecond. The stuff disappeared, but not before shedding a phantom particle: a positron where an electron had been, an antiproton where a proton had been, a gamma-neutron where an ordinary neutron had been. The antiparticles destroyed more of the contained matter, producing more energy, more particles accelerating to the speed of light and disappearing. The creation of the phantom particles? All a matter of topology. Where were the accelerated particles going?

Imagine another . . . call it dimension, universe, continuum, what you will. Whatever it was, it was smaller than this one of ours, they were sure smaller not in terms of dimensions, for that concept had no meaning. Smaller, say, in terms of the amount of available free energy it could contain. A young universe, perhaps, a continuum with a point-for-point congruency with the real universe if you accepted the postulated geometry for this other plane, with an inverse entropy as far as we were concerned. The available free energy of that micro-universe could increase. That's what was happening to the partitioned energy. The particles, traveling faster than light, were carrying it elsewhere and dropping back into the real continuum turned inside out the way you turn a glove inside out. The available free energy of that micro-universe was greater than that of ours for a given . . . could you say . . . volume of space. There was an energy incline. If you reversed the field as the unfortunate German had, well . . .

You weren't creating energy, though. You had already, through a decade of experimenting, poured energy into this other place, and the reversal of the field merely released it. Just a matter of two continua seeking equilibrium. (Perhaps, as someone pointed out, the very operation of the first Black Field had created this other place. No matter, it was there and the effect could be used.)

The Black Field offered two possibilities. Controlled fusion or the Artery. A long-term gamble, with the certain price of failure a collapsing technology if you were willing to invest the money and the massive labor of building the Artery. The deposits of U-235 as the hydride had been discovered on Pluto, but it wasn't commercially feasible to bring the metal back by ship. The fleet of freighters needed alone would have severely taxed the metal resources of three worlds, not to mention that the energy requirements for such a commercial flight were such that you'd be lucky to achieve a 10 percent payload.

Gamble on the development of controlled fusion? With the world starving for power, with space flight itself hanging in the balance, with the populations of one-quarter of the world on a minimum subsistence diet after the past two decades' debauch of using Terra's fissionable resources at a drunken rate? The nice thing about the Artery was that there was a near-inexhaustible supply of power to run the accelerator and the other equipment right on the site. Why worry about how much U-235 you consumed, just so long as you didn't have to burn the stuff in a ship?

End result? Hearings following hearings, Bayerd leading them along, explaining, cajoling, meeting the attacks of the Patel faction, seeing always the massive vision of a band of metal stretching from far Pluto to the Earth, pumping in new life. Adrianne Patel had called the concept a "Goldbert." The solution Bayerd was proposing, she said, was so complex that the expenditure of effort in another direction could find a simpler solution. Only she wasn't sure of just what that solution would be.

Even during this period Bayerd had seen a great deal of Adrianne Patel, even though now they had become friendly rivals. No longer was she in his camp, helping him with the project. Still he was not the sort who could put aside that special relationship they had developed just because she opposed him in this particular area.

On the Shrenk deck he paused and pushed from the chair, floating through the air, drifting for a moment in nothingness while his thoughts considered that far period. How had they become lovers, he wondered. He was far too obsessed, too concerned with this project that would assure his fame to be that concerned with the usual human relationships. He had taken her with his group originally, and eventually as his third in command, because of her remarkable mind, her ability to cut through useless details to the core of a problem. For a long time it had not occurred to him to think of her as a woman. Indeed, it was during that period that he developed the habit of calling her by her last name, as though that staccato word somehow removed her from the province of women.

Still, it had happened in the most casual and matter-of-fact fashion. She had wanted him from the start, Bayerd now realized, and had set about in a bold and reasoned way to become a part of him. The thought that she could have been so pragmatic now angered him. Then he was flattered . . . distracted, but flattered. He supposed that everyone knew about it, but in his ignorance he thought that he might pull it off without a breath of rumor.

When she told him that she was going to have his child, he became angry in a fashion he had never allowed himself to be. He wanted no extraneous problems then to interfere with his work. He couldn't understand how it had happened until she told him quite matter-of-factly that she had planned it that way, that she had taken no precautions simply because she wanted his child.

Yet, in spite of his anger, he had grown more and more proud as the time approached with a kind of primitive awe that his loins could magically spawn another being. In time, he supposed he might have gloried in the idea of fatherhood, had the child lived. It was obvious from the start that the child's delivery would be Caesarean. Its position was wrong for one thing, and nothing succeeded in changing that. Even without that it might have been necessary because of her size and the narrowness of her pelvis, with her almost boyish hips.

Through all this, she remained the independent self-contained woman. When he, still schooled in the somewhat backward mores of the midwestern United States, where he had grown up, insisted that she marry him, she merely smiled and brushed him off. This was her baby, and beyond his initial contribution, she was determined that it would be her undertaking. At first he rather respected her for it but, as time grew and they began to disagree on the necessity of the Artery, he began to resent her independence. Still, he was, he supposed, in love with her. Certainly he was concerned about her. Their final break came some two months before the birth of the child.

Gilchrist was just a fledgling commissioner then, out to make his reputation in the jungle of world politics. He was the first successful scion of Irish farmers and as scrappy and violent as that troubled land in which he was reared. Somehow he obtained a copy of a long, technical memorandum Patel had authored in which she questioned the growing problem of controlling the Artery. She had also made a most telling case for investing the money in two areas: an attempt to bring the technology of breeder piles to a level that would meet power needs, and a crash effort on the laser-induced fusion reaction, coupled with the new Black Field technology. To the layman the arguments were telling and persuasive.

Bayerd had been furious, quite beyond any anger he

had ever felt. That Adrianne was a part of what he had come to look upon as a betrayal made it all the more terrible. The Artery had become for him a personal symbol.

"It's become your key to immortality," she accused him.

"Who else would have the daring to conceive of such a project?" he said angrily.

"The daring or . . ." she searched for a word, "or the hubris?" she asked. "Norm, I'm more and more convinced that this is not the way to go."

"So you go behind my back and make common cause with that jackal?"

"I had nothing to do with the leaking of the note," she said.

"Which I'm quite prepared to believe, you think?" he snapped.

In the end many other words were said, words not easily forgotten or retracted.

After that he thought of her as the Enemy. Still, she carried his child, and he could not forget that. He consulted his attorneys, trying to find some way in which he could gain possession of the child if it were a boy. He wanted a son very badly. If it were a girl, he would not be particularly interested, but a boy . . . a son to hand this grand vision to. Perhaps he was being selfish, but he had become obsessed with the magnitude, the grandeur of the Artery project. He saw every opposition as part of a concerted plot to oppose him. He remembered the high emotional state of the period in which he would at one moment be totally elated at some new success, some special mention of him and his vision in the news services, to be followed by the blackest depression when he found opposition mounting or . . . worse . . . when, in spite of himself, he began to have doubts. He could not allow himself doubts. He had to remain fixed in his purpose, his eyes clearly on his objectives. No doubts. Above all else, no doubts.

He sealed the doubts away in some separate corner of his mind. He ceased to acknowledge them. It were as if he had become two personalities, one a driving, demanding person bent on this penultimate achievement, the other frightened and doubting and filled with the sort of masochistic self-loathing that he had always despised in other men.

When she was taken to the hospital, McDow called him at his office. He was due to appear before the Appropriations Committee within the hour, but he forgot this completely in the sudden alarm that she might lose the child. She was not due for another month, but this sudden emergency could cost him the son he wanted so badly. He rushed from the building into the streets and nearly overheated the engine of his monopod in his anxiety to get into traffic.

They had taken her to a subhospital in the north part of the city. This alone added to his sense of alarm. Apparently they had not found the time to rush her across town to the more elaborate Commission facilities, where she was scheduled later that month. The traffic was particularly heavy and the afternoon drizzle compounded the low clouds of acrid smog drifting in from the Jersey countryside. Several times he narrowly avoided collisions, illegally activating the vertical on the craft several times. His panel was glowing repeatedly, the computer noting the traffic summonses that were being logged against him as he turned up the broad stretches of Gamal Boulevard and gunned the turbine.

He had no warning of danger. The twenty-wheeled lorry beside him swerved to avoid another monopod, and its mass struck his passenger compartment. The whole pod literally ripped itself from the engine and undercarriage. He was suddenly turning head over heels, the pod twisting like a live thing as it flew through the air. The rending of metal and the quick shards of flying plastic were the last thing he remembered as a heavy something struck him at the base of the skull.

He did not regain consciousness for nearly two months. They had carefully kept him in hypothermia while they repaired his shattered body. When he was finally released, they told him,

"You're lucky. You came out of that without a scratch."

"What about the baby?" he asked.

"Adrianne's fine," McDow told him.

"That's not what I asked," he said.

"They did everything they could," he said, watching Bayerd's expression closely.

"She lost the child?" he demanded. McDow nodded.

It seemed as if a chill fog had descended over his mind. He was without emotion, not even a sense of tragedy. The child . . . the son-to-be was gone. He supposed that for some time he blamed her for it, but eventually even that emotion faded in the new wave of intensive work. They had the appropriation, and the project was under way. They established the computer stations on Pelambang with the subsidiaries in

New York and Amsterdam. The construction of the Black Field station began almost within the month and was well advanced when he began to have problems with faintness and fatigue.

They checked him over repeatedly, puzzled and unsure of themselves. Finally, they spotted the blood clot that had formed at the base of the brain and the resulting scarification.

"A millimeter more," the doctor said, "and you would have died in tetany. We still can't handle the complete loss of the pituitary."

"What do you mean?" he demanded.

"The scarification. It appears to have involved the posterior lobe of the gland. That's why we put you through the drill with the oculist. We thought at first it might be a pituitary tumor, which means it would press on the optic nerve and be readily diagnosed in that manner. Sometimes they're operable, of course, but it's rather a clumsy operation. One comes in through the roof of the mouth and . . ."

"Damn it," he said. "What does it mean?"

"Well, we can give you glandular supplementation," the doctor said, "but we're concerned with the function of the adrenals. We still don't understand the full complexity of their operation. My colleagues think it might be Cushing's Syndrome."

Which it was, of course. There had been some question of hyperthyroidism at first, but the intensive tests had shown a profound overproductivity of the adrenal cortical hormone. They had tried several ways of modifying the gland function. Theoretically, the medications available should have controlled its function, but for unknown reasons the cortex failed to respond. They tried selective radiative destruction of part of the cortex, but the technique was dangerous and they had finally confessed failure.

The progressive muscular weakness had come upon him more quickly than they had predicted. Fortunately, he had been able to transfer activities to the Black Field Station. Now, of course, any return to Earth except for a yearly medical checkup was unthinkable. He would be completely incapable of operating under Earth's gravity, just as he needed the prosthetic chair for the low-'g' environment of the bridge. Fortunately, he thought with some irony, they had solved one problem, the heavy deposition of melanin in the skin that had gradually turned his normally pale coloring into a series of ugly blotches. That they could control by a drug that broke up the chromopores.

He shook himself from his reverie. No need for another exercise in self-pity, he told himself. He moved into one of the vacant Shrenk cubicles. It was the cubicle assigned to Gilchrist, he saw. He found the monitoring tapes with their time codes and carefully ran the last one back to the hour of transmission, searching for the telltale hiatus in the impulse that would indicate a shift to another Shrenk robot. He searched on either side of the spot that marked 9:00 but failed to find any indication of a jump. As nearly as he could determine, the councilman had occupied the robot on the Needle for the entire period after the tour that Elliott had shepherded through the plain installations.

He moved from the room and entered the next one. In quick succession he checked the cubicles belonging to Mendoza, Beckworth (who had not used his in days, since he had no direct concern with operations), and finally Elliott's.

He paused outside of the vacant cubicle assigned to Adrianne. All at once he knew that he would find the solution here. It had to be here. Who else had a better motive for destroying him? He felt the rage buried within him beginning to stir again.

And he remembered that she had not been on the Needle when he had returned. She had been wandering somewhere below, completely out of sight of the members of the Needle group, out of sight of the crew below on the plain. How simple, when she saw Bayerd's robot go lax, to switch to the abandoned body, make the changes in the capsule in seconds, and leave?

He pushed open the door, feeling his heart pump. A part of him protested, but he went ahead. He knew what he must surely find there.

Van der Reis was terribly frightened. He had been half awake when it happened. He recalled the lights suddenly glowing in the ceiling of his room, the last image of Carmelita half through the irised door, her eyes wide and fearful. Then the terrible wrenching feeling as he seemed to fall into a deep, cloying darkness.

He was tumbling, head over heels, his head swimming with dizziness. Nausea came then and a terrible desire to retch, a desire that found no relief. His eyes generated flashes of color, but there was no color, only the complete sort of blackness that humans rarely experience, a blackness that was the absolute negation of light.

Then his senses were flooded with images. He seemed to be seesawing back and forth from one scene to another. He saw faces, distorted and fearful, several of them with mouths wide open as though screaming. Then blackness again, followed by a wave of intense heat. He opened his eyes and then closed them tightly. Someone was gasping and screaming, and he realized as his chest throbbed that it must have been he. For an instant it seemed that he were in the center of a great fire, perhaps the heart of a sun. The image scarcely impressed itself on his brain before he was again falling through space into the ever-present blackness.

He hit a cold, hard surface. He lay, moaning, trying to recover his breath. The adrenalin weakness invaded his limbs and he pressed himself into the cold surface. Finally he opened his eyes slowly. He was laying on a black ceramic surface that seemed semitransparent to a depth of an inch. Within the surface tiny glints of gold sparked and swirled. The stuff seemed for all the world like a piece of obsidian he had once seen with the frozen golden flow lines deep in the volcanic glass. Only these flow lines were not frozen. They swirled and moved in a manner he had never seen.

He rose slowly to his feet and looked about. The floor under him curved laterally to join the wall of the same material. The walls in turn curved over his head. The immediate area in which he stood was of elliptical cross section, but stretching to the front was a curving passage of the same obsidian material that altered its shape, flowing into other complex forms. He turned and found that the passage curved away to his rear in the same manner.

There were no features to the passage, nor could he

see more than twenty meters in either direction. He stepped out cautiously, and very nearly lost his balance. The curved surface under him was like ice, with a remarkably low coefficient of friction with his boot. Moving his feet carefully, he began to walk. Ahead of him the constantly changing passageway stretched into the unknown.

Akira Fusaka pulled the bedroll tightly around his body and shivered. He opened gummed eyes to the early-morning light and checked the brazier by his side. The charcoal had slumped into a feathery gray ash, but the ceramic bowl still radiated some heat. He reached out into the chill morning air and secured some scraps from the coarse bag near at hand. With one of the charcoal sticks, he stirred the coals dropping the feathery ash through the grate and exposing red live coals. Then he stacked charcoal on top of these and waited for moments until the glow began to spread from the old coals to the new fuel.

The sun was not yet up, but it was light enough to make out his surroundings. In the far corner of the warehouse in which he slept were stacked bales of dried vegetables and kelp, while close at hand were bales of furs that the Ainu had prepared for shipment. His questing hand touched the cold metal of the carbine beside him. The chill suddenly reminded him of what had brought him to the warehouse the previous night. He had returned to his hut to get the weapon, even though common sense told him that the light 0.25-caliber round would be insufficient to stop such a ponderous animal as the cave bear. Still, it gave some comfort.

He consulted his watch. It was now nearly eleven hours since he had called in his report. The prefectural magistrate had assured him that he was dispatching a platoon of men to take over Fusaka's responsibility. Knowing Sugiyama, the aging magistrate, Fusaka was sure that the men had been rousted from their warm beds and were probably on the way already. Sugiyama had the reputation for being a martinet who delighted in making the men assigned to him uncomfortable.

Fusaka pulled himself from the bedroll, throwing back the heavy cotton quilt, and stretched. He had slept with his clothing on, but he had removed his boots. These he now proceeded to warm above the brazier, wrinkling his nose at the odor of heating rubber and canvas mingled with the older body scent. Finally they were warm to the touch, and he put them on. Then he made for the door of the warehouse, wondering if the impossible beast were still trapped within the crude cage.

Kawakami was nowhere to be seen, and the area around the cage was completely deserted. During the night snow had drifted up about its base. He came over and looked inside. In spite of the light, the interior of the cage was dark, with the darkness assuming an almost physical presence. He heard a sleepy growl and knew that the beast was still there. His hand strayed to the bandages on his chest and he felt again that fear of the night before. Carefully, without getting too close to the cage, he scraped away the snow before the door with the butt of his carbine. Peering inside, he could make out a vague massive shape, huddled in the corner. The beast was silent now, glaring out at him with white, feral eyes. He shuddered, thinking how quickly that great mass could become a razor-clawed engine of destruction.

He stepped back to inspect the cage just as a group of men rounded the far side of the warehouse. There were seven of them, six soldiers in double file commanded by a sergeant. Kawakamisan brought up the rear, his cotton robes trailing in the snow. The men were all wearing canvas dress with heavy quilted overjackets and helmets. The sergeant yelled, "*Tomare yo!*" and the men come to a halt. The sergeant approached Fusaka, his boots with the separated toe pounding the ground and raising a flurry of powdery snow.

Fusaka waited patiently until he halted. Fusaka bowed. The sergeant clutched his side arm and bowed stiffly in turn. "You are Fusaka-san?" he asked. There was a touch too much arrogance in his voice, Fusaka noted and he frowned disapprovingly. After all, he was not a peasant to be spoken to in such a manner.

"You are correct," he said, using a pronoun that clearly set the sergeant in his place. He could see that the man in turn was annoyed.

"I am Gunso Okamoto," the sergeant said sternly. "The prefectural magistrate has ordered me to investigate a wild story about a great beast."

"It is true, it is true, gunso-san," Kawakami said, bustling up. "My people captured it in the great cage."

"Humph, let us see," the sergeant said and stood forward. Fusaka turned and led the way as the sergeant scurried in an attempt to get ahead of him. He was certainly not going to let this pipsqueak of a homeguardsman get the better of him, Fusaka promised himself.

The three of them paused before the great cage. The sergeant leaned forward and peered inside. Fusaka thought of warning him but decided that he could take his own chances.

"Careful," Kawakami said. "Careful, gunso-san. The beast is dangerous when angry."

"What beast, old man?" the sergeant spat. "There is no beast inside your silly cage."

"It comes and goes," Fusaka said.

"That is foolish," the sergeant said. He used the wokd *bakarashii*, which brought sudden color to Fusaka's face. "There is no beast. It is all an old woman's tale to frighten children to bed," the sergeant said. He began to paw at the bindings on the cage door.

"Wait," Fusaka said.

"I have no time for such nonsense," the sergeant said. "Let us see what mouse you have trapped in your great cage so that I can report back to the prefecture."

As he swung the cage door aside and started in, Fusaka grabbed at him. He had seen what the sergeant had not, that first flickering in the blackness, the sudden resolution of the giant form. The sergeant pushed at him and he was falling forward . . . forward suddenly into the waiting arms of a horror of fur and teeth.

He cried out and tried to regain his balance. The thing lumbered forward. Behind him, the sergeant fell back with a cry of disbelief. In the next instant Fusaka felt himself seized, not by an animal paw but by strange constricting forces that seemed to buoy him up as water buoys up a swimming body.

Before him the fog-laced morning light flickered, and waves of backness rushed in on him.

In Pelambang, Martin had just left Carmelita and was making his way up to the corridors into the restricted memory banks. He had transferred some of his activities to this area now that van der Reis was no longer around. He had never understood why Karl made such a secret of this area, for the memory complexes were much like those to which he had access in the rest of the station.

He paused in his optical robe, suddenly listening. He stood between four of the memory units that filled a room twenty feet square. Beside the new units, still unactivated, these were dwarfs. Moreover, their capacity per cubic meter was a whole order of magnitude lower than the newer units.

He was not sure that he had heard. At first it sounded much like a distant whistling . . . no, rather a soft rush of air, as though someone were opening a compressed gas bottle. He paused, puzzled. Then the other sound burst upon him. It sounded like a wild animal, angry and shouting its rage as it attacked. He was quite unprepared for what happened next.

In the center of the units a black something flickered into being and out again. He had a quick impression of some great beast that was all talons and teeth and blazing eyes. The thing appeared again, and before it, half crouched as though falling forward, the figure of a small man. He was clad in heavy clothing with a quilted cotton jacket. The beast was moving forward at a clumsy cant, its great paws reaching out for the sprawling man. The masses of the two figures intersected several of the scanning beams. Had they been optically neutral, very little would have happened, but the sudden reflection of the beams back into the memory matrices was disastrous.

Martin had no chance to key an override circuit. In the next minute overload lights were flickering against the far walls, and a keening whistle sounded its warning of whole memory sections wiped out and others shorted into nonprogram responses. There was no smoke or visible signs of disaster, but in the instant he knew that a good portion of the memory capacity of the station had been expunged from the memory cells as though it had never existed.

In the next instant both man and beast disappeared, leaving the space between the banks as empty as it had been moments before. Martin watched as the scanning systems died and the override panels, now silent, flashed their endless red warnings. Too late now, he thought with dull futility.

Bayerd pushed open the door to Adrianne's Shrenk cubicle, knowing with a quiet dread what he would find there. The room was clothed in darkness except for a red glow-panel in the ceiling. He moved to the monitor unit, found the tape, and began to rewind it to the spot that had recorded the instant when her hate and resentment of years had proved too much, when she with a quick movement of a switch had usurped the body by the capsule and condemned millions to disaster . . . to death.

In the dim light he inspected the tape. It was there! The tiny hiatus where the Shrenk unit had been switched to another robot body. And the time was 9:00.

For a second, he felt somehow depressed. The reaction was completly anticlimactic. This was the evidence he had been seeking. Yes, the index along the edge clearly established the time. The taped record would show which robot on Pluto she had activated. Bayerd need only run the tape back on the reel and play back the coded data. He leaned forward to inspect the sound track running parellel to the data track, wondering what sounds Patel must have unconsciously voiced in that instant of betrayal. In the next instant intense pain lanced through his temples.

It felt as if someone had hit him with a steel bar. There was a suffocating something over his mouth, cutting off air. Swirls of color raced before his eyes as his body tensed. He felt his muscles snapping with the effort, trying to fight upward to consciousness.

He felt something crushing his lips inward, smothering him, and he tasted the warm taste of blood before he fell into the smothering darkness . . .

Chapter Eight

H PLUS ELEVEN HOURS

He was wrapped in pale light while a part of him stood apart and watched the endless drifting of his body. There was something at the farthest range of his vision, separated from his living self by great distance, by light-years even, that was approaching him with fantastic speed.

It would only be a matter of minutes . . . seconds

. . . days . . . years . . . time until it were upon him and all thinking, all feeling would cease.

Drifting in an eternity of soft light and warmth with the touch of chill on his back . . . soft light and formlessness . . . and he knew that he could not leave in this manner with no form, no substance on which he might pin some memory of his past existence.

Drifting, he searched the light in which he moved and saw that he was enclosed in a fragile sphere whose boundaries were sharp and well-defined . . . that beyond this sphere of light, the endless black, flecked with bright stars, stretched to infinity, and there was nothing that would carry him outward from his sphere of radiance to those other far spheres of light. There was only hereness and nowness and that soon to be dissolved . . . by somthing moving toward him with incredible speed, something cold and stifling and smothering and . . .

Somewhere dimly he heard a voice and he felt something drawing him upward. He fought against the pull, seeking only to drift silently in his tiny universe of light apart from the thing rushing down upon him. He looked far out, and then he saw it.

Like a great sable curtain sweeping through space, blotting out the stars. A vast mass of utter lightlessness that swallowed his universe. But there was a speck of light that grew in a long parabola racing across his pool of brightness, and he knew that it was a thing upon which he might fasten and that would bear him ever outward to those distant universes before the endless black curtain would enfold him in its stifling substance.

He sent his consciousness outward in all directions, seeking for something. For a stone, a twig, a shard of metal with which he could mark the place where he had been . . . where in the night that would quickly fall, someone finding it might know that he had been there and had afterward gone hence . . .

But there was the pull, something binding him to the spot and pulling him upward . . . upward into greater light . . .

Into brilliance and . . .

He opened his eyes to whiteness. It was seconds before he realized that he was staring up at the woven fabric of a sheet, through which an overhead light penetrated. He threw the sheets from his body and saw that he was lying fully nude on the bed.

No, not he. Rather another body, full and well-muscled, young and virile with deeply indented pubic fold and heavy, hairy thighs. For an instant he was completely disoriented. Then he recognized the body, just as he heard her splashing in the sonic shower in the fresher room.

"My God," he said aloud.

"I thought you were asleep already," he heard her say. "Is the light bothering you? I can mute it."

She came from the shower, her dark skin red and glowing from the sonic-water blast. She was drying herself with a great fluffy towel, being rather seductive in the way she rubbed the cloth over her body. How beautiful, he thought, and then the panic hit him again.

"What am I doing here?" he demanded.

"Why wouldn't you be here?" she asked, coming to the edge of the bed. With a sudden abandon she threw the towel to the far side of the room and pirouetted before him. "Do you like me?" she asked.

"Oh God," he said. "I don't understand it. I can't be here, not here in this body."

She frowned, looking suddenly worried. "You haven't been yourself this past month," she said. "Something's troubling you. Is anything wrong?"

"Wrong?" he laughed. "You couldn't appreciate how wrong. It doesn't make sense."

"I know what makes sense," she said. She jumped, knees first into bed, and began to rub his chest. With growing wonderment, he realized that he could feel her fingers, feel the stirrings of hair under the palms of her hand.

"This is insane," he said, shaking off her touch. "One minute and then . . ."

And it all blacked out, all faded from view.

"Norm," someone said, "Norm, what's happened?"

And there was a warm arm supporting him, buoying him up and away from the bright radiance, away from the onsweeping blackness to . . .

Light as his lids faltered open.

The room was a mass of shifting shadows. He felt a deep throbbing pain behind his eyes and the blood pulsing frantically in his temples. There was a tight burning sensation in the pit of his stomach and his muscles felt lax and drained of energy. He struggled into a sitting position as McDow said, "Are you all right?"

He shook his head, trying to speak, but his throat was tight and his mouth dry. For seconds he couldn't manage a sound. He wet his lips and swallowed. He felt the astringent taste of blood in his mouth, and his exploring tongue told him that in his struggles he must have lacerated his own cheek lining with his teeth.

"I think so," he said at last. "It all happened so fast."

He tried to get to his feet and fell back against the

metal bulkhead. For an instant sharp pain shot through his temples. His exploring hand found a throbbing area at the back of his head.

"You were gone almost two hours," McDow said quietly. "I began to wonder and came down to find you."

"Where's Adrianne?" Bayerd asked.

"Up in Commo. She's been handling the message traffic on the operations we set up."

"Has she been there all the time?"

"Why, yes," McDow said. Then his brow wrinkled in thought and he said, "That is, I suppose so. I've been busy on the metering bridge. She's been in Commo every time I came down, though. Why? You don't think . . . ?"

"I don't know what to think," Bayerd said, getting unsteadily to his feet with McDow's help. "I know one thing, though."

He made his way, supported by McDow, to the monitoring tape unit and removed the spool.

"Hit the lights, will you?" he said.

McDow touched the induction plate by the door, and the walls and ceiling glowed a soft radiance. Carefully, Bayerd rolled the tape from one spool to the other, searching again for the significant area of the tape. After a few minutes he realized that something was wrong. The break was there, but the time code was not the same. The break was now coded at 9:05.

"This isn't the same tape," he said. "Someone's switched it for the original."

"What's so important about the tape?" McDow asked.

Bayerd told him. McDow whistled and said, "Are you sure?"

"Damn it, of course I'm sure. I was hunting for just such evidence when I started checking the monitor tapes. It isn't likely I would make a mistake."

"But this means Adrianne was the one who changed the capsule settings."

"It looks that way."

"I find that a little hard to believe."

"Don't be a fool," Bayerd said impatiently. "It's hard to believe about anyone, but she is one of the most likely. Only I can't prove it now."

He passed a hand over his eyes. The hand, he noticed, was shaking, the tips of the fingers vibrating with tiny tremors. His jaw muscles ached as though he had been holding his teeth clenched for a long time.

"You'd better get Doc Beckworth to check you over," McDow said, reaching out a hand to steady him. "Give me the tape. I might be able to find something in the coded data."

"You're welcome to it," Bayerd said. "It's probably pretty crude. She didn't have time to do a good job of faking."

"Let's go," McDow said.

"All right, but the story is that I fell and banged my head. No one's to know about this for the present."

"I'm more concerned at the moment with another problem," McDow said. "We've had a communications blackout from Pelambang for nearly an hour."

"What are you doing about it?" Bayerd demanded, massaging his scalp tenderly.

"There's very little we can do about it," McDow said tiredly. "Whatever happened down there, we've lost direct computer tieup."

"Not now," Bayerd said. "Above all, we need that tieup in the next few hours."

"Let's get your head taken care of," McDow said.

They found Beckworth in the dispensary down the corridor from the Commo room.

"What happened to you?" he demanded as Bayerd settled his chair to the desk.

"Never mind," bayerd said. "I fell over my own feet. Just patch up this bump and take a look at the cut inside my mouth." He turned to McDow and said, "Go on to Commo and see if you can help Adrianne. You might look into that other matter as soon as you find time."

"Right," McDow said, checking his watch.

"How much time?"

"Less than two hours to first contact," McDow said.

After he left, Beckworth examined the wound on Bayerd's scalp, carefully clipping away a small circle of hair with a pair of surgical scissors.

"That's a nasty bump," he said. "Looks like somebody clouted you one."

"Maybe someone did," Bayerd said wryly and then, "Ouch, take it easy, will you?" He felt moistness as Beckworth followed the antiseptic with a thin layer of topical antibiotic ointment over the wound. He sealed the wound with a thin sheet of porous protein film, which would eventually be absorbed into the open tissue, and touched the button that rotated Bayerd's chair backward.

"Open your mouth," he said. He took a small pencil

light from an instrument tray and examined the wound on the inside of Bayerd's right cheek.

"How the blazes did you do this?"

"I told you, I slipped and fell."

"You've chewed a hunk of flesh the size of a dime out of the lining," Beckworth said. "The edge of the tongue is lacerated too. Could give you a nasty infection."

He eyed Bayerd speculatively.

"You didn't do that in a single fall," he said. "Want to tell me about it?"

"Damn it, Doc," Bayerd said. "It's none of your business. Get the damage patched up and don't ask so many questions."

"And you can go to blazes too," Beckworth muttered under his breath as he secured a swab from a sterilizer. After he painted the interior wound and affixed two tiny plastic lamps with a forceps, he handed Bayerd two yellow capsules and a glass of water. "Tetracycline," he said. "We'll try to keep the bugs away from that fevered brain."

"Thanks," Bayerd said tiredly. "Look, I'm sorry about snapping your head off. I've been working under a lot of tension."

"Are you sure that's all?" Beckworth asked.

"What other explanations should there be?"

"Wait a while. There are a few checks I'd like to run through."

"Save it," Bayerd said. "I haven't got the time."

"You'd better take the time," Beckworth said. "From the looks of you, if you don't, we'll be taking you back Earthside on a stretcher."

At the door to the dispensary, he said, "I'm sending you back anyway by the first shuttle after this mess is cleaned up. I want a complete checkup on you, and this is one time I'm going to get my way, even if it does mean a week flat on your back."

"Your privilege," Bayerd said.

Adrianne Patel turned from the communication bank and said, "Well, that's the story."

"What could have happened?" Mendoza demanded.

"More important," Gilchrist growled, "how complete is the erasure in the banks?"

"From what Carmelita tells me," Adrianne said, "it's fairly complete. Of course, most of the programs are already stored in the new bank."

"Perhaps they could reprogram from them?" Mendoza suggested.

"No, I don't think there's enough time," she said tiredly. "It makes more sense to activate the new banks."

"Isn't that dangerous?" Mendoza asked.

"Of course," she said, "but there seems to be little choice. Unless Norm overrules them, they'll have the new banks tied into the computational array in less than an hour. They won't be operating at full capacity, but for our purposes they'll be quite adequate to do the job."

Gilchrist snorted. "Always patch, patch. You'd think this whole Artery Project were being held together with tape and wire. I'm surprised, Mendoza, that you can still believe that the Artery is a viable system when something as small as this spells out disaster on such a scale."

Mendoza colored. "The concept is sound. You know that, even if for your own purposes you won't admit it. What's happened today would just as easily have happened in one of your hypothetical fusion stations. You talk knowingly about containing a productive fusion reaction, initiating it with a laser and using the Black Field to assure yourself that what happened on the Isle of Man won't happen in a populated area. At this level of complexity, all technology is potentially dangerous."

"Gentlemen," Adrianne said, "please let's not waste our time on useless recriminations. The Artery exists. That's a hard fact of life, and the Artery now represents a potential danger to an unknown number of people. That's the first order or priority, and nothing else should interfere."

"Bravo," Bayerd said ironically, jetting his chair forward through the back hatch. "Nobly spoken. You should be commended on your idealism."

She stared out into the blackness beyond the station, only her sudden stiffening showing that she was aware of him.

"That's not necessary," Gilchrist said. "She's right, of course. We may have disagreed, but we have a common enemy now."

"I'm sorry," Bayerd said, feeling not at all sorry. He was angry, and in spite of himself he felt a growing rage for this woman who had betrayed him in the past and was now probably responsible for the disaster facing him. "Have you re-established contact with Pelambang?" he asked after a moment.

"Just a few minutes ago," Mendoza said. "I don't fully understand what they're up to but . . ."

"They've reported an 80 percent loss in redundancy in the memory banks," Adrianne said. "Unless you have a better solution, they're going to activate the new banks."

"Are you sure they can't transfer the programs?" he asked.

"There isn't time," she said.

"How are the two intercept groups coming?" Bayerd asked, ignoring the statement.

"The *Ingrid* has a pickup mounted to give us a picture of the operations," Patel said. She touched a plate before her on the desk, and the wall screen flickered. The image of the *SAU-62* slowly formed. It was a half-silver sphere of two hundred feet diameter with a thick tubular leg and two smaller open girder frames extending rearward to support the thrust units that expelled the heated hydrogen.

Four smaller points had clustered about the *SAU-62*, which was drifting slowly away from the screen. The ships were all of the corvette class, Bayerd saw.

"It's a touchy job," Adrianne said. "The Karmanship's shape is a clumsy one to handle, and they don't dare try for more than half a 'g' acceleration."

"Can they get into position in time?"

"I think so, but then they've got to build up the skin charge. We'll position the corvettes nose to nose in a cross to balance their thrusts, cut out their charge dissipators, and build up a skin charge on each ship by throwing out as much ionizable mass as fast as possible. Then we'll bleed the charge away through a cable to the inner surface of the *SAU-62*'s hull. The charge will migrate to the outside surface immediately, of course, which will allow us to build up quite a charge density without worrying about electrostatic repulsion too much."

"What about beam data?"

"The *Ingrid* will be standing off with a bank of ultraviolet-sensitive 'strob' units. She should catch the beam angle with an error of perhaps 5 percent. Certainly no more."

"Do they have Shrenk bodies aboard?" he asked.

"Two," she said. "Do you want to take over one?"

"Of course," he said.

"McDow the other?"

"No," he said slowly. "It's strictly an observer function. He's needed here. I think I'd like you to take the other."

"Me?" she asked in some surprise.

"I suppose it's my sense of the ironic," Bayerd said bitterly. "Whether we intercept the beam or not will determine the outcome of our separate stands. It seems appropriate that you be there in person." He winced and touched the bandage on his head.

She noted the gesture with widened eyes, but said nothing.

"What about the group at the belt? The *CX-248*?"

"I can't get a picture on them yet," she said. "The captain of the cruiser *Orion* is handling that end. They're decelerating the *CX-248*, but she's buckling badly."

"Let's hope they get that polyparalene bag out intact. Can you give me the details on the charge density they can develop with that thing?"

"I'll check on it," she said.

McDow had entered as they talked. He leaned over now and said, "Norm, the news is out Earthside."

"What do you mean?"

"We've just received a telecast from below. There's rioting in New Delhi, Stuttgart, and Boston."

"I radioed back," Gilchrist said belligerently. "No reason to hide the fact. If I hadn't, you wouldn't have taken any measures to minimize the disaster."

"Councilman," Bayerd said slowly, "it's difficult for me to tell you just how many varieties of idiot you are. There's absolutely nothing that can minimize the potential disaster in the short time we have, and your little political maneuver has probably cost thousands of lives just from the resulting panic."

"I don't take that sort of talk from anyone," Gilchrist snapped.

"You'll take it from me, mister. I'm damned tired of having you underfoot." He turned to McDow and said, "All right, we'll be very proper now and declare this a military emergency. Escort Councilman Gilchrist down to his quarters."

"By God, that's just about enough," Gilchrist roared.

"It is indeed," Bayerd said. "Now get below quietly or . . ."

Mendoza placed a hand on Gilchrist's shoulder. "Let's go," he said softly. Gilchrist glared at Bayerd and then bowed slightly, his face twisted in a crooked smile.

"In a textbook situation," he said, "the little martinets always win. This isn't the end of it though." He withdrew with Mendoza as McDow said, "He did that deliberately."

"Of course," Bayerd said. "He wants a panic to dramatize the issue in the Council." He turned to Adrianne. "Why didn't you stop that idiot?"

"I'm sorry," she said. "He must have got to the radio while I was away from Commo."

Bayerd beckoned McDow aside as Beckworth entered and walked over to Adrianne. "Check that tape thoroughly," he told McDow, "and get at the message tapes here in Commo."

"Why?" McDow asked. "The message had gone out already."

"Yes, and it was sent while Adrianne was away from Commo. If we can get a time on the message and it coincides with the time I tripped over my feet downstairs, well . . ."

McDow nodded in understanding.

"Right now," Bayerd said, "I want to check on the work at the capsule."

"Anything else?" McDow asked, looking at Beckworth and Adrianne. Beckworth was handing her a message flimsy and explaining something to her in low tones.

"No," Bayerd said slowly, watching the other two. He wondered what Beckworth was sending. It was probably in med administration code, and he couldn't find out by checking the tapes later. He had a strong suspicion of what the message was about. Why, he thought, didn't the meddling fool leave things alone?

"I'm going to check out with the Plutonian crew," he said, turning his chair toward the hatch.

"What happened to your head?" Adrianne asked.

He told her, minimizing the accident. He made it sound as if it were a matter of clumsiness. She eyed him suspiciously but said nothing.

As soon as Bayerd had left the deck, Adrianne busied herself with the pickup controls for the *SAU-62*. She glanced at the message flimsy tacked to the magnetic board at one side and wrinkled her brow; Beckworth had used some sort of interstation code that made no sense to her. Finally she turned her seat and said, "Doc?"

"Yes," Beckworth said. "Is there something bothering you?"

"You know there is," she said. "Norm appears to have had some sort of accident at just about the time that the Pelambang computers went out. If he were in contact through Shrenk robot, he would have known the full story before we did. He seemed not at all surprised when I told him."

"I don't understand what you're saying," Beckworth said.

"It would be quite an emotional shock," she said slowly. "I've wondered quite a bit about his physical condition. You know, he had a rather severe skull injury years ago."

"I'm aware of that," Beckworth said coldly. "I have his complete medical history. In fact, that's the main reason for my being on the station—to see that he stays in good health."

"That seems very strange. I know your background, You were a specialist in myogalvanic linkages. Before that, you were an encephalographist."

"That's true," he said slowly.

"Doc," she said suddenly, "is Norm an epileptic?"

"What makes you ask a thing like that?" Beckworth demanded angrily.

"The sudden blackout. I noticed his lip was stained very much, as if someone had been treating a lacerated tongue. There have been other incidents earlier in the history of the station. Gossip gets around."

Beckworth shook his head slowly. "It's true," he said, "that a severe head injury can bring on a history of seizures, but I can assure you that such is not the case with Bayerd. He has no history of either *petit* or *grand mal.* His encephalogram gives no indication of such a possibility. I've practically lived with his medical history for several years. It's strictly out of the question."

"I get the impression," she said slowly, "that you're protesting a bit too much."

"Not at all," he said. "On my word of honor, there's no possibility of epilepsy in Norman Bayerd's case." He came over to her and placed his hand on her shoulder. "Are you really that concerned about him, I mean, personally concerned?"

"It's hard not to be," she said, "even after all these years. You didn't know him then, the bright and eager young man who was going to reshape the universe in his own image. He had the sort of appeal a woman can't ignore, a kind of virility that comes from too much life in one body."

"That's a very poetic statement from the woman everyone has described to me as a cold and political animal," he said.

"We tend to draw within ourselves as we get older," she said. "I suppose I have too. It's still very much a man's world out there in spite of everything. To compete you have to lose some of what makes you a woman. Not everything, however."

"I suppose I'd be prying if I asked you if you still love him," Beckworth said.

"No, not prying. It's a futile kind of question. It's hard to say whether after many years you love someone or whether you love the image you once had of them. I still see the Norman I knew in moments when that rigid reserve of his weakens. That part of him I love. You know, we were going to have a child once."

"Did that make the difference? The loss of the child?"

She smiled bitterly. "That's a question I can't properly answer," she said. "No, no, I don't think that made the difference with me. It went back before that."

"Take a word of advice?" Beckworth said slowly.

"Of course," she said. "At least I'll listen."

"I can appreciate how you feel. It's a part of romanticizing one's past life and emotional attachments. In this case I would very carefully put it out of my mind."

"I've been trying that for some years," she said.

"I sincerely hope you're successful," Beckworth said.

She turned to the board, noting that Bayerd's Shrenk cubicle was now activated.

On the way down to "S" level, Bayerd moved with a feeling of numbness and fatigue weighting his body. He was going to have to rest shortly, he knew. He was pressing himself close to the limit of his endurance. As he entered his cubicle, he thought: *Please, God, just let me finish this last piece of work. Just this last and then it doesn't matter what happens.*

He thought of the vast chaos sweeping whole continents. Of the cities crumbling under the shock wave, the vast unheard sound toppling bridges, shattering the steel and concrete of buildings, and the screams of the millions who would die in the short instant the beam penetrated the atmosphere and shed its energy in the fantastic compression wave that would grow from the livid wound in the air.

He pressed the thought down with quick panic and

lowered himself into the Shrenk harness. He sat for long seconds, trying to gain control of his body, which was suddenly wracked with a thousand small quiverings of fear.

His hand touched for a moment the hidden panel that would have hurled him back to Earth to that secret body he had visited only an hour before. No, that was a mystery he would have to probe later. How had he come to be in that body in the few moments (or was it an hour, as they said) of unconsciousness? Perhaps he had not been truly unconscious, but had managed to stumble into the Shrenk harness and activate the distant body. Had indeed living that distant life with Elen, who had fled from her metafamily to his arms, become so important that in moments of stress he would unconsciously flee to it?

He shook his head, wondering at the contradictions within his own personality. Then he thought of Adrianne again. Cold, implacable woman, and yet so capable of warmth and love and that special caring that he had always valued in women. For a second he sighed with the feeling of loss. If it were only possible to retrace all those lost years, to find some way of explaining this pressing need of his to her. No, she would react in much the same way, and the whole tragic misunderstanding would play itself out again.

Better to forget it, to deaden that small part of him that still found pleasure in seeing her under the pain and resentment. He thought of Elen on Earth again and realized that much of what had attracted him to that vibrant girl was her resemblance to Adrianne. No, not the Adrianne he had known but a simplified version, quite content to be a woman and to hold her man by the devious methods women had been practicing for eons. None of this constant need for personal confrontation to demonstrate that she too was a personality in her own right. Perhaps he was being medieval in his attitudes. Certainly few men of today looked for a woman with the peculiar characteristics that he had wanted. Perhaps it was a reflection of his overriding ego. God knows, she had accused him of that often enough in jest. (He realized years later that she had not been joking, that she found his insistence on a dominant male role the one single corrosive feature of their affair.)

He touched the panel before him, thinking that it would be so easy to flee this responsibility. Of course, that too was naïve, for how long could he hide in that secret body with his true self forever trapped here in the station? There was no escape, he told himself. For him there was never an escape. He had built a prison for himself almost from the day that he was old enough to think, and that prison, coupled with his disease, had now been fully realized in the station and the Artery.

Sorrowfully, he activated the Shrenk unit and made the movements that hurled him in an instant over five light-hours to stand on that dark Plutonian plain.

Means had called in the local police and two hours later had asked for additional support from the Home Guard. They arrived within the hour, two flitters of them, almost a full company with side arms and electric prods. In spite of this the crowds before the computer installation grew hourly. The news had spread quickly since Gilchrist's initial news release to the services. Before that, only scattered newsmen and the usual hangers-on had appeared before the low fences, their worried shouts easily ignored by the personnel inside the building complex.

Now, the Guard was having difficulty in restraining the crowds. Many of them had already seen the newscasts from abroad and knew that this scene was being duplicated around the globe, regardless of the hour. In Bombay, Tel Aviv, Paris, New York, Chicago, Rio de Janiero, Mexico City, similar crowds gathered before government installations, their impatience transferring itself to the embattled officials inside the buildings that served the Artery.

Carmelita and Martin had come to the roof for a breath of air after the initial emergency of checking out the storage losses in the old banks and the decision to activate the new ones. Below them in the interior of the building, harried technicians now scurried through lightless corridors, checking out the makeshift circuitry that would tie the new memory banks into the over-all computer complex.

Carmelita looked over the railing down at the crowds surging against the tightly locked ranks of the Guard. She shivered and moved close to Martin who, quite without realizing it, put his arm about her. At another time she would have resented the intimacy, not that such was not allowed in their arrangement, but because it would have been an unconscious symbol of male ascendancy. This, above all, was a direct violation of the rules the metafamily lived by. Tonight, she felt the need for some kind of comfort and assurance.

"It's all right," Martin said quietly. "A few hours and it will all be over."

"One way or another," she said.

"Enough of that," he said. "It is no use to think negatively. The changeover to the new units is going well, and all the preliminary tests show that they will function properly."

Below, a sudden surge of the crowd pressed against a part of the Guard line, and men began to shout as the Guardsmen unlimbered their electric prods. The crisp morning air was filled with the sound of curses and then sudden blows as several Guardsmen went down under the rush. The surging mass of confusion sorted itself out as more Guardsmen from the reserve rushed forward and clubbed at the attackers with their prods. Carmelita gasped as several of the civilians went down under the feet of the guards.

"Let's go below," she said.

"Don't worry; they won't get through," Martin assured her.

"What would they do if they did?" she asked.

"I don't know," he said. "I don't understand what they hope to accomplish."

Below, the amplified voice of a man . . . Carmelita realized after a few words that it was Means . . . began to shout calming phrases. ". . . No emergency . . . everything is under control . . . go to your homes and wait for news . . . the emergency is under control . . ."

"Let's get some coffee," Martin said. She nodded silently, and they walked to the levitator. On the way down, Carmelita asked,

"What about the Omicron banks? Can't we use them as a backup to the new banks, as a sort of a cross check?"

"No," Martin said, stepping from the levitator into the corridor. "We have enough redundancy. Besides, I have very particular orders about that set. It's not to be touched under any circumstances. Very top secret from Karl."

"Oh," she said, making a face. "In all the press of work I had forgotten about him. That's terrible of me."

"Don't worry," he said gently. "If there is a way, we'll get him back."

"But from where?" she asked.

"I think, given another few hours of work, I can answer that," Martin said. "If there is an answer," he added. He put his arm around her, and in the privacy of the corridor, she suddenly began to weep.

"He was very good to me," she sobbed.

"Was that enough?" Martin asked, confused by the sudden surge of emotion within himself.

"Enough?" she said. "What is enough?"

"Perhaps," he said, kissing her gently, "perhaps that is something that we can never know until we experience it."

Chapter Nine

H PLUS FIFTEEN HOURS, THIRTY MINUTES

The obsidian corridors seemed endless, their shapes constantly changing as van der Reis cautiously explored them. Because the curvature was uneven, he was unable to estimate just how large the featureless place was, or indeed if he were not doubling back on his own trail. Occasionally he passed lateral passages, rather like spokes in a wheel. Still he kept to the main passage for the moment, putting off the exploration of the lateral passages until he was sure that he had indeed circumnavigated the structure.

He had been unable to blaze a mark on the hard, glassy walls, but he tore a sheet from his pocket notebook and dropped the crumpled ball of paper on the curved floor at one point. After wandering for over half an hour, he had not yet come to the paper again. From his estimates of the curvature of the passage, he knew that he should have returned to his point of origin by now. He considered the complex surface over which he had been walking. Was it possible that there was a slight downward tilt to the surface? It was hard to determine because of the way the curvature kept changing, but if this were so, he might be walking through a spiral, or worse, a helix. In the latter case, he would have no idea just how far the passage extended.

He finally paused at one of the spokes and considered his prospects. He was surprised to find how fatigued he had become. At first he ascribed it to the extra effort in walking over the curved, slick surface. He sat down to rest. Something about the way his body behaved as he lowered himself to the cold surface surprised him. He took a stylus from his tunic and watched as he dropped it from overhead. Mentally he counted as the instrument hit the black surface and rolled. Yes, there seemed no doubt about it. The stylus had fallen too fast. Not so significantly that he could be absolutely sure without a stopwatch, but he had expected a rapid count of two to three, but the stylus hit the surface between counts one and two.

He raised his hand experimentally and felt the tension in his biceps. Was he imagining it? The arm felt unusually heavy, as if it had increased in weight by perhaps 25 percent. That would make the acceleration of gravity in this place over 1200 cm/sec^2. No wonder he was feeling so tired. At Pelambang his usual weight was 80 kilograms. That would mean that he was now bearing a weight of at least a hundred kilos on his frame. He was surprised that he had not noticed it before.

He rose to his feet, testing his weight. Yes, there was no doubt about it. The pressure around the ankles, the feeling of heaviness in the torso. He wondered if he were still on Earth. The air in the passage was fresh and breathable, but that did not necessarily signify anything. He realized suddenly that there was a definite current to the air and that a distinct breeze was blowing from the spoke passage near which he sat. If that was the source of the air, he should certainly explore it, he decided. Nothing further was being accomplished by this endless walking down the curved corridor that might go on for miles, or (the thought was frightening) might double back on itself in the manner of a Klein bottle, leaving him forever trapped on a topologically infinite surface.

For an instant, panic seized him, and he found that he was shaking badly. A feeling of loss welled up in him as he thought of Carmelita and Martin and the others. In this nightmare he had somehow been spirited away from them, and he wondered if he would ever see them again. He rose to his feet and shook off the mood. No time for such self-pity, he told himself. He started for the spoke passage near him.

He had just entered the passage and proceeded along its length perhaps five meters when he sensed a sudden blast of air from the rear. He whirled in time to see a shimmering presence suddenly appear in the passage he had vacated. The image quivered with specks of light and seemed to gain substance as he watched. In the next instant he realized that it was a human figure, tumbling head over heels into the passage, appearing from apparently thin air.

The small man in quilted jacket fell to the obsidian floor and sprawled there. Van der Reis saw that he carried a carbine held by a web sling to his shoulder. His garments were loose and baggy cotton, his shoes an odd mixture of canvas and what appeared to be rubber. The toes of the shoe were separate, as though the big toe were oddly articulated.

Van der Reis must have gasped at the apparition, for the man suddenly sprang to all fours like a cat, and then stood erect. He looked wildly about as he pulled the carbine from his shoulder. He was bleeding from several cuts on the face, van der Reis saw, and his jacket was shredded in spots as though from the claws of a wild animal.

The man struggled to his feet and looked wildly about him. He was small and wiry. There was something wrong with one of his legs, van der Reis saw, that caused him to move awkwardly.

Van der Reis called out, "Are you all right?" in English and the man suddenly looked at him.

"*Eigo!*" the man gasped, and before van der Reis could say anything further, the small man raised his carbine. His Oriental face twisted into a scowl as he fired. The carbine round whipped past van der Reis and he heard it ricochet several times off the curved black walls, its high whine sounding like some Earthbound demon.

"Damn it, stop it," he yelled.

The man fired again. He was obviously shaken from his experience, or his aim would have been better. There was little choice. Van der Reis ran forward, covering the distance between them in a second. The man reversed his carbine to use it as a club as van der Reis hit him. They tumbled into a heap and began to struggle. The carbine skittered across the curved floor.

"You maniac," van der Reis yelled and hit the other man in the chest below the sternum. He fell back gasping.

Van der Reis crouched for a new attack. He was panting badly, and he knew that he must beat the man quickly before the relative difference in their ages worked in his opponent's favor. He threw himself forward on the man. The man rolled, and he hit the floor hard. In a second the Oriental was on his feet, looking wild and aiming a kick at van der Reis. Van der Reis grabbed his foot and he stumbled back into . . .

Into the embrace of a raging horror.

Van der Reis did not know where the beast had come from. It seemed to appear as had the man, its great hairy bulk looming above them. It lips were drawn back in a phosphorsecent snarl that exposed yellow foam-flecked teeth. The small man beat futilely against the beast.

Van der Reis did not hesitate. He ran to the carbine, checked to see that he knew how to operate it, and raised it to his shoulder. The small man had somehow pulled away from the bear, but the beast was lumbering forward toward the man's sprawled figure. Van der Reis pulled the trigger and pulled it again. He saw tufts of hair fly from the point of impact, but the beast continued. It turned and came lumbering toward him, ignoring the sprawled man. Van der Reis emptied the magazine at the horror and then realized that he could not stop it with the weapon. In the last instant before the razor-sharp claws touched his body, he knew that he would not be able to flee.

Bayerd had lost all track of time in the subdued frenzy of the work about the capsule site. There was little he could do except watch. Long ago he had schooled himself to patience after he had given an assignment. The crew working below to cut down to the capsule were doing as much as they could under the difficult circumstances and, if he were tempted on occasion to relay an instruction down to them, he held himself in check, knowing that this would only disconcert them and inevitably slow the progress of the work.

Once McDow called him on the command net to tell him that the new banks in Pelambang were now checked out and would be in full operation by the time the beam front reached the *Ingrid* and the *SAU-62*. He should have felt a lessening of tension after that, he told himself. Everything that they had learned about the beam heading and the size of the static charge they could develop in the Karmanship assured him that they would be successful in deflecting the plasmoid stream. In a matter of less than an hour it would all be over.

There was still the problem of the capsule, sealed under tons of rock. Progress had been slow, but Chang was optimistic at this point. In the last half hour, they had hit a spongy layer where escaping gases had foamed the rock, and the going had been much easier. When this emergency was over, he reminded himself tiredly, there was still a great deal of work to restore the Artery and begin transmission. He shuddered at the outcry on Earth when it became known that the beginning of transmission might be delayed another thirty days. Still, he could not conscientiously promise any more. There remained a great many things to check out, even after the capsule was restored and new calibrations set. Then, he reminded himself, there was still the problem of the unknown saboteur. (Unknown? Somehow he still couldn't believe that it was she.) This was of pressing importance. He could, of course, exclude Adrianne and Gilchrist from the station and that would, he supposed, solve the problem. But what if she were not responsible? Suppose Chang or Muletti or Trubner or even McDow were somehow responsible or any one of the Plutonian crew? He couldn't afford to take the chance. The one who had tampered with the capsule setting had to be unmasked definitely before he could safely entrust the transmission again to the automatic equipment.

McDow's voice cut into his reverie: "Norm, thirty minutes."

"Right," he said and radioed a few last-minute instructions to Chang, who presently had charge of the crew in the pit. For an instant he stared at the Needle, thrusting up from the pool of shadow that was the fissure circling the outcropping. It seemed as if the lookout point were floating on a sea of blackness with the cold stars blazing intensely about it. He had not realized until this minute how completely isolated physically and symbolically the Needle was from the immediacy of the Artery and its installations on the plain.

He withdrew to the Shrenk cubicle in the Black Field Station, seated himself in his prosthetic chair, and made his way to the Commo Bridge. Adrianne met him at the hatch, her eyes wide and worried. "They're cutting it awfully close," she said. "They'll have barely twenty minutes to build the skin charge up to strength."

"That's time enough," he said gruffly, and then in spite of himself he thought better of his tone. "I'm sorry," he said. "I'm pretty tense."

"We all are," she said. Then, "After this is all over I'd like to spend some time talking."

"What's there to talk about?" he said. "We spent a lot of time talking years ago and it didn't seem to matter in the final analysis."

"I haven't been completely honest with you," she said. "There are a great many things I should have told you."

"Not completely honest," he said in mock astonishment. "You? Not completely honest. Truly, that is a statement that amazes me."

"You and your stupid pride," she flared and turned away from him.

Bayerd jetted his chair past McDow and Mendoza, who was staring at the screen with an intense fascination. The image on the screen was being transmitted by the *Ingrid*, and the Karmanship took up almost a quarter of the image. The ship was very large. It consisted of a pair of paraplene spheres each over a thousand meters in diameter, their fragile structure expanded on a light metal mesh. The spheres were transparent, but half of them had been silvered. The working load of the ship was positioned between the great spheres ahead of a large tank of liquid hydrogen. The ship worked on the greenhouse principle. Radiant energy entering the transparent half of the spheres was reflected off the silvered area, but the resulting radiation could not again escape from the sphere and thus raised the temperature of the gases within the spheres. The gas was hydrogen from the reaction mass chamber. The gas expanded against the tough paraplene and was vented through expansion nozzles that used the energy of the gas to propel the ship. The resulting thrust was fairly small, so that the maximum acceleration of the ship was an order of magnitude lower than the simpler plasma ships, but the acceleration could be applied constantly, and over a period of months, truly astonishing velocities could be imparted to the ship. It was an ideal vessel for transporting low-cost materials that were not immediately needed or were not perishable. The ship normally carried a complement of two crewmen, since it never ventured closer than five hundred miles to a planetary surface and practically ran itself.

The four corvettes had grouped around the *SAU-62*, tethered at the ends of long cables, their exhausts flaming green and blue. At a distance from the motors a hazelike fog expanded. Colloidal aluminum, Bayerd thought, realizing that they had cut off their water injection systems, so that the metal, after passing through the MHD acceleration chambers, was being ejected in its elemental form. The clouds were dispersing rapidly, since each particle carried a like charge and tended to repel adjacent particles.

"We'd better get the Shrenk harnesses if we want to observe this close up," Bayerd said.

"I still think I should go with you," McDow said uncertainly.

"No, I've already made that decision," Bayerd said. "Adrianne, are you ready?"

"I really don't . . ." she began and then resignedly, "Very well."

On the way down to the "S" deck neither of them spoke. Bayerd found himself perversely pleased that she would accompany him. As soon as they had deflected the beam segment, she would have lost. He wanted to see her face when she realized that the Artery was safe and that everything would be exactly as it was before. He stole a glance at her as he left his chair in the free-fall area. She seemed worried and very tired, and for a moment he felt his heart soften for her. She carried her age well. She was still the woman who had so attracted him those long years ago. A part of him thought sorrowfully how sad it was that they could not have joined hands and lives as they planned instead of having evolved into the most implacable of enemies.

When they activated the harnesses and found themselves in the Shrenk bodies aboard the *Ingrid*, the captain was waiting for them. "Commander Bayerd," he said saluting.

"I am Bayerd," Bayerd said when he realized that the captain could make no distinctions between the bodies.

"I'm Captain Johanssen," the man said. "We have perhaps ten minutes to contact time. I would suggest that we move quickly to the bridge."

They followed him along a metal passageway floored in soft plastic, and up a short levitator column. The bridge was located on the periphery of the vessel so that they could look out directly through a wide, vitreous port without resorting to viewscreens.

"My astrogator and chief engineer have set up three strobe units on the exterior of the ship," Johanssen said. "We'll be able to photograph the beam as it passes and get three readings for a further plot."

"How many frames will you take?" Bayerd asked. "You must remember that the beam is traveling at a quarter 'c.' "

"We'll start running the pickups in five minutes," Johanssen said. "If luck is with us each unit will pick up between thirty and fifty frames of the beam. That should certainly be sufficient."

Outside, the array of ships presented a bizarre sight. The four corvettes had been positioned at the end of four cables so that their thrusts were balanced. The cables led through ragged holes in the spheres of the Karmanship and were affixed to the metal framework inside. As the charge built up on the corvettes it was conducted along the cable to the interior of the spheres. The electrons immediately migrated to the exterior of the spheres, accumulating minute by minute to build a massive static charge.

"Do you have a reading on the charge density?" Bayerd asked.

Johanssen said something to his engineer and then said, "We're 40 percent over the calculated density. If you've calculated the beam path with the accuracy you claim, this will do the job." He glanced at the ship chronometer. "We've activated the monitoring strobes. We'll see how successful we are within the next thirty seconds."

It was at this point that the structure holding the

two great spheres of paraplene collapsed. The strain on the light titanium structures must have been tremendous. There was little warning. The small lateral acceleration added to the already overburdened structures was enough. The two spheres seemed to leap away from each other, collapsing as they did. Bayerd saw a faint cloud of moisture erupt into space and freeze instantly. The whole structure was wobbling badly and moving laterally at an unexpected acceleration. In the last few seconds, he realized that the sudden venting of hydrogen under several atmospheres had been sufficient to impart a significant velocity to the light structure. The result had been a slackening of the tension on the cables and a sudden realignment of the three remaining corvettes so that their thrusts were now roughly aligned in the same direction. Even as they watched, the cluster moved out of sight.

"Quick," Johannssen said, "turn the ship."

In the depths of the *Ingrid*, hidden inertia centers roared suddenly, and the ship slowly changed its orientation. The cluster of four corvettes and the collapsing Karmanship drifted into view.

"Get them back into position," Bayerd roared.

"There is nothing I can do," Johanssen said, clutching at the console before him. "They've moved in closer to the predicted path. Perhaps it is not . . ."

He did not finish the sentence.

The Karmanship suddenly bloomed in a fraction of a second into an expanding flower of brilliance, its center the cargo pod between the buckling spheres. An instant later the corvettes were engulfed, and the expanding wave of brilliance engulfed the *Ingrid* . . .

Bayerd was on the "S" deck, his body trapped in the Shrenk harness. Instinctively he knew that the distant robot body had ceased to exist, and with it Captain Johanssen, his crew, and the *Ingrid*.

He hit the switch of the command net and yelled, "For God's sake, McDow, what happened?"

"I don't know," McDow said. "The ship's pile perhaps."

"No," Adrianne's tired voice drifted over the net. "It was something we did not consider. The ship's cargo was air for the Callisto Experimental Station. Oxygen, nitrogen, helium, hydrogen, the normal spectrum of gases. Plus, of course, carbon from the paraplene spheres. The heat from the beam . . ."

"A carbon-nitrogen reaction," Bayerd gasped.

"Yes, it appears so."

"But," McDow said, "that means the same thing will happen if the beam touches the Earth's atmosphere."

"I'm afraid you're right," Bayerd said sickly.

Chapter Ten

H PLUS SIXTEEN HOURS

He crawled from the Shrenk cubicle, his weakened muscles quivering with the sudden flood of adrenalin. It had been rather like dying a second death, he thought, being on the *Ingrid* in the instant it was snuffed out by the expanding radiance. The thought of Johanssen and those other men suddenly vaporizing before the wall of fire made him sick.

"Norm," Adrianne said, coming from her cubicle and placing her arm gently around his shoulder, "Norm, it's all right."

"All right," he said. "My God, all those men gone."

"It wasn't your fault," she said.

"Whose fault was it?" he demanded. "Whose fault was it that the beam transmission failed in the first place?"

"No one's," she insisted. "It was a malfunction, something you couldn't have avoided."

He looked at her in horror. Surely, some flicker of emotion would betray her, some element of guilt would find its reflection on that smooth face. To have caused the death of so many because of a simple political difference. No, the one who had sabotaged the beam must have recognized the inherent danger in what would happen. It had taken a cold and completely amoral intellect to contemplate such a crime. If it were she, then she would not betray herself. Could she have changed so much, he wondered.

Or, he thought, did I ever really know her?

She helped him into his chair and they made their way upward to the communications bridge, where McDow and Mendoza awaited them silently.

"What happened out there?" he demanded. "Just when we thought that everything would be fine . . ."

"One of the corvette motors failed," McDow said. "You saw that. Then the Karmanship buckled. They'd built up too much of a charge. Well, hell, the superstructure was never built to take that kind of stress."

"What effect did we have on the beam?" Bayerd demanded.

"I'm waiting for Pelambang," McDow said. "We monitored the *Ingrid* sensors right up to the moment they were vaporized. That means that we may have enough frames to plot the beam path after it triggered the ship's cargo."

"Surely you can't be correct," Mendoza said. "I know I haven't the background, but it seems impossible that gas under that pressure, that concentration, could have sustained a phoenix reaction. What about the cross section?"

"Well, it wouldn't sustain the reaction," McDow admitted. "What we saw was the result of perhaps a half percent conversion at most. The inertia of the gases would allow that much reaction before they began to expand away from the center. After that, of course, the capture probability would drop to the point where the reaction couldn't sustain."

"Whatever the degree of conversion," Bayerd said, bitterly, "it was enough to destroy every vessel in the immediate area."

"No," McDow said. "One of the corvettes survived. We've received signals from it. I don't know how long it will take to get a rescue vessel to them."

"How much air do they have?"

McDow shrugged. "They lost their reserves. They'll have to depend on their recycling equipment."

"What's the crew?"

"Twenty men," McDow said.

"They'll never make it," Bayerd said. "Not unless they lose half of the complement."

"That is what they're debating now," McDow said. "It's a rotten situation, but it isn't the first time this sort of thing has happened."

"Horrible," Adrianne said, shivering.

"Yes, isn't it?" Bayerd said fiercely.

"How much chance do we have of stopping the beam now?" Mendoza asked.

"Our only hope now is the *CX-248* and that group of ships near the asteroid belt," Bayerd said.

"But we'll need a greater deflection," Adrianne objected.

"I don't understand," Mendoza said.

"At that point the beam will be scarcely an hour and a half from intersecting the Earth-moon system," McDow explained. "To miss the system the beam path must be deformed a significantly greater angle than at the point where we tried to intercept it with the *Ingrid*'s group."

"If our data are correct," Bayerd said, "we should be able to get close enough to do that."

"God knows, it was remarkably precise a few minutes ago," Adrianne said. "If the ship hadn't drifted into the path of the beam, it would have passed within a hundred meters of the Karmanship."

"Can we depend on that degree of precision?" Mendoza wanted to know.

"Of course not," Bayerd said. "Being that close was something of a fluke, and the precision drops with the distance. If we can get good sighting data from the *Ingrid*'s sensors, however, we can predict the path with the degree of accuracy we need."

Mendoza said slowly, "I dislike saying this, but even if you do deflect the beam, there's still the problem of the sealed capsule on Pluto. In not too many hours transmission will begin again automatically, and you have no control over the direction of the beam. We may well be facing the same problem over again, but on a greater scale."

"What can we say about that?" Adrianne asked. "Do you think there's still a chance that they will get to the capsule in time?"

"Truthfully, I don't know," Bayerd said. "They've been hurrying as fast as they can, but the work is slow."

"Something drastic has to be done," Mendoza insisted. "I think we should try explosives."

"No, we can't risk damaging the accelerator," Bayerd objected. "We've been over all this before."

"Nevertheless," Adrianne said gently, "it doesn't appear that Chang's group is making any appreciable progress. After they cut through the spongy area, they encountered an even denser layer, and that has slowed them appreciably."

"We can't afford to risk the accelerator," Bayerd insisted. "If the accelerator is destroyed, it is doubtful that our power reserves can hold out long enough for us to build another. You forget what a tedious engineering job it was in the first place."

"It may be the only solution," McDow said slowly. "Forgive me, Norm, but it may reduce to a choice of falling back to lesser power sources or seeing the Earth literally destroyed by an uncontrolled transmission."

"I hate to say it," Mendoza said. "There seems to be no other choice but to use explosives." He turned to McDow. "You'd better give the order," he said.

"Just a minute, Councilman," Bayerd said angrily. "This is still my command. If there are orders to be given, I'll give them."

"This is on my own responsibility," Mendoza said.

"I'm not in the habit of shifting responsibility when it belongs to me," Bayerd snapped. "All right, this seems to be the general opinion. I don't agree, but at this point I can't offer an alternative."

"You can't gamble that they'll reach the capsule in time otherwise," Adrianne said.

"Very well," Bayerd said to McDow. "When we've reached H plus 19, give the order."

Without waiting for an answer, Bayerd directed his chair through the hatch and down to the "S" level to his quarters, which were opposite the Shrenk installation.

He felt as if he were living a dream. His head ached from the scalp wound, and his exploring tongue found the inside of his cheek raw and tender to the touch. The weight of the last few hours pressed heavily on him, and he knew now that he could not go on without some rest.

There wasn't much he could do, he thought, as he entered his small sleeping chamber. He pulled himself onto the web hammock, drew the counter webbing over him, and secured it to insure that, in this low-weight area, a chance movement would not throw him out of bed while he slept. Then he lay for a long time staring into the darkness and savoring the cool breeze that blew over his face from the air-conditioning duct above his head.

What difference did it make, he thought, if Adrianne had been the one who changed the capsule settings? It was too late now for recriminations, too late for accusations or revenge or . . .

No. She had tried to destroy the Artery, rob him of the product of his life, destroy the place he had built for himself in the advance of man to the stars.

Only . . . only she had said that he had pressed mankind into a straightjacket with the Artery, that humanity had entered upon a period of stasis, of arrested development simply because it took every bit of its energy to survive at the present level.

Never get beyond this system, never go to the stars? He couldn't believe it. The drive was too strong.

Only what had been done in that direction in ten years? Had there been any major advances toward a stellar drive? There had been a thousand and one refinements of existing techniques, but the significant breakthrough . . .

That wasn't right. The Artery represented the life of Earth. Without it she would never have come the distance she had. Nothing . . . disgrace, death . . . nothing could stop him before he proved that. Least of all death, he thought.

He thought again of those long summer days so many years ago. Would he ever rid himself of this cloying sorrow that the conscious part of his mind rejected? What might have been. God, those words were the worst the human race had ever invented. Had it not been for the accident, he might have eventually brought her around to his way of thinking, but the accident had taken him out of action for months. The forces he had launched with Mendoza had proceeded with the inevitableness of their own inertia. When he was again conscious of the outside world (they had kept him under complete sedation for months, it seemed), the project was a funded fact and the forces captained by Gilchrist had admitted defeat. The accident had been another kind of defeat for him, he thought dreamily. Imprisoned on this tiny man-made world, he might as well have lost the great gamble of his life.

Why couldn't it have been a quick death, he thought? Better than this waiting, this secret knowledge of the seeds of death lodged within him . . . better to . . .

No, every hour, every tiny instant was important to secure this thing he had built from the assaults of people like Patel. . . . What had she said on the Needle those long hours ago, something about the Artery and pyramids?

Well, the Artery was a momument those ancient pharaohs might well envy in place of their useless masses of ritual stone. "I met a traveler from an antique land who said. . . ." What was that? Shelley? She had once asked him if he knew "Ozymandias." "My name is Ozymandias, king of kings. . . ." Small, egotistic man who thought of the world as that tiny speck of sand about a muddy river and died, thinking that the stars were bits of fire set in a bowl over his head if he bothered to think about them at all. "Look on my works, ye Mighty, and despair. . . . Round the decay of that colossal wreck, boundless and bare. . . ."

That was the whole clue to her thinking. Destroy the Artery because the Artery was the symbol of his life, and . . . well, face it . . . the symbol of his virility, his potency as a man.

Was that what had menaced her? He would not have believed it at one time, but she had grown more poised and self-sure in the years . . . more masculine in her way of thinking, he admitted. No, damn it, the idea was too classical, too Freudian, and no one believed in Freud any more or in the thousand subsequent students and hangers-on. Still, how could a woman truly love a man whose visions were so monumental that the very manhood she wanted was concentrated in this incredible achievement?

" 'Look in my works, ye Mighty,' " he quoted in his sleepy mind.

" 'Ye Mighty and despair!' "

Only there was a poem . . . he dimly remembered it . . . by Hopkins. What was it, "The Leaden Echo," that ended in that word: "despair." Only to be followed by "The Silver Echo," which began, "Spare!"

Spare? What does one spare in such a battle? One's self? Never. Least of all he had spared himself. And he thought fiercely as his mind drifted into sleep, it had been well worth it.

Hadn't it?

Adrianne Patel left the bridge shortly after Bayerd and proceeded down to "R" level where the visitors were quartered. She thought of going to her quarters for a short nap, but decided against it. Instead she paused at Gilchrist's door and finally buzzed the annunciator. His harsh voice came immediately, "Yes?"

"It's Adrianne Patel, Councilman," she said, and moments later he was ushering her into the small two-room suite.

"I thought you were in the camp of the enemy," he said.

"I've been trying to help," she said. "This is something I can do quite well, you know. That's been one of my chief advantages in your campaign, understanding the technical details of the Artery installation."

"I didn't mean that the way it sounded," he said,

offering her a drink. "It's just that this infernal minor god of yours annoys the hell out of me."

"Bayerd?" she said, finding a seat and trying to be comfortable in the low gravity. "Norman Bayerd is a very frightened man," she said. "That's why he's reacting in the way he does. You would too if you carried the weight of responsibility he has carried for so many years."

"You've always been ready to find some apology for him," Gilchrist accused, smiling ironically into his drink.

"I suppose so," she said. "I understand him probably better than anyone in the world. Oh, I know, he's pig-headed and opinionated and reacts like a tiger when someone crosses him. Truthfully, I suppose that was why I first found him so attractive."

"Yet, you've cut him off completely. You've never let him share any part of your life, even that part that was uniquely the product of you both."

She colored angrily. "You know, we agreed never to speak of that. That's a part of my life that you have no concern with."

"I'm concerned about you in every way," Gilchrist said gently. "I don't want to see you hurt. You were hurt badly once and you had the courage to withdraw before you were hurt more."

"Oh, yes," she said, "I had courage, if that's what you call it. Perhaps it was just that I was too tender, too afraid of the pain in trying to force commitments."

"I don't suppose you've ever considered telling him?"

"That his son didn't die? That he's still alive? No."

She shook her head sadly. "No, that was a decision I made some time ago. Can you imagine what terrible battles we would have waged for his love, had Norm known? It was a decision I made with a clear conscience. You can have a clear conscience when you set out upon deception on such a scale. Still, I think I did what was best for him."

"And what will Bayerd do, now that his grand monument is toppling on his ears?" Gilchrist demanded.

"Do? He'll do whatever is necessary, whatever he conceives his duty to be."

"Even to utterly destroying the Artery?"

"I think so," she said.

"I wish I could believe you," Gilchrist said. "It may well be that eventually we on this station will have to take things into our own hands."

"No," she said. "No, that's the last thing we should do. He's not a madman, not even a good first-class paranoid. He's a man obsessed with an idea, but if the idea fails him, he'll discard it just as easily as . . ."

"As easily as he discarded you?" Gilchrist offered.

"Yes," she said. "Yes, I suppose that's what I mean."

"I don't share your optimism," Gilchrist said, pulling himself to his feet and holding to a stanchion above the liquor cabinet. "I wish he had that unpredictable quality that makes human beings do what you least expect of them, but I fear Norman Bayerd will do just what we may expect of him."

"No," she said. "No, that's not true."

"You're still very much in love with him," Gilchrist accused.

"Oh, I don't know," she said, half in tears. "I don't

know. I see him and remember his tenderness, what a marvelous thing it was to be with him and to feel him against me in the nighttime."

Gilchrist wrinkled his brow in thought. He was obviously in the throes of some difficult decision. Finally he said, "I repeat that we may have to act unilaterally if the situation worsens. That means destroying all or part of the Artery installation."

"I couldn't allow you to do that," she said. "Not while Norman thinks . . ."

"While Bayerd thinks there is a chance. You see," he paused, then seemed to come to a decision. "You see, the operative phrase there is 'Bayerd thinks,' but there is a doubt in my mind that the phrase applies."

"You speak in riddles," she said.

"I don't mean to," he said. "I think perhaps it's time I told you a very important piece of information. It's probably something known to perhaps ten people. Beckworth, van der Reis, certainly McDow, a few others. I'm not even sure that Mendoza knows it. I came to it by a very involved process."

"That complex intelligence operation of yours," she said.

"Well, yes," he said. "You can't operate in the midst of a political complex like the Council without some personal information-gathering service. One of my men came across the records on this case while checking back on a period when Bayerd was out of the hospital, sometime before he was announced as officially discharged."

"You make all of this sound pretty ominous," she said irritably.

"It is," he said. Then in slow and careful phrases he

began to tell her what he knew. She listened with growing horror, scarcely breathing, knowing intuitively that what he told her must be true . . .

Van der Reis was frozen in horror at the apparition lumbering toward him. Never in his most terrible nightmares had he seen such a thing. The beast opened its wide jaws, and cascades of saliva dripped from its great teeth. Its paws stretched out, reaching for him. In the last instant, his feet lost their paralysis of fear and he turned to run. The beast was on him in the instant, its great arms enclosing him in a crushing grip.

He pulled back and felt claws like knives ripping his clothing and the flesh of his abdomen. He grabbed at his belly and stared at the blood welling between his fingers. There was no pain for seconds; only the terrible feeling of torn tissue. Then pain welled over him and he realized that he was badly hurt. He had no time to investigate; the beast was lumbering forward again. In the background, he heard the Oriental yelling something, but he could think only of fleeing.

He turned and began to run. He had taken barely ten steps when he slipped and fell to his knees. A wave of pain seized him, and for a moment he thought he might vomit. The other man was yelling excitedly and he turned to see the cave bear halt and raise itself to its full height, its muzzle sniffing the air.

The things came drifting down the black corridor. There were three of them suspended in midair without obvious support. For a moment he thought they were machines and then, in spite of their odd shape, he realized that they were organic. Not human, but certainly living. One raised an appendage, and a pale red flame seemed to leap from the end. It spread and enveloped the great bear. The beast roared its fury and then abruptly winked out. It were as if someone had been projecting a lantern slide of the beast and had simply turned off the projection lamp. One second the bear was there, and in the next second it had ceased to be.

Van der Reis panicked. He stumbled to his feet and began to run. The shining black corridor curved about him. He was in one of the spoke passages, and this ran arrow-straight into blackness. His feet were slipping rapidly as he ran because the floor curvature in the spoke passage was more severe than in the main corridor. Ahead of him a light-swallowing blackness loomed. He plunged into it.

The shock of transition was too much. He was suddenly in a cylindrical room with four hatches. The floor was quite flat and the walls were welded steel. He fell back against one wall trying to catch his breath. His belly was sending raging signals of pain. He clutched at his wound and tore aside the cloth. His abdomen had been completely torn open, and he could see the loop of an intestine protruding. Around this, blood pulsed in bright red gouts.

Somehow he had to get help. From those things in the corridor? He shuddered, and stumbled to one of the hatches in the curved wall. The operation was obvious. He touched a silver plate and the hatch slid aside on lubricated bearings. He felt suddenly dizzy. He tumbled through the hatch and onto a flat, unprotected walkway. He had tried to avoid falling on his face, and his hip and shoulder struck the metal surface. Then he rolled slightly and looked down. His sudden gasp of fear tore through his body.

He looked into emptiness. Far below him he could see broad swards of vegetation, half obscured by mists. In the distance many miles away but visible from his height a pastel city seemed to hover above the mists. Below him, a black pillar arrowed to the distant ground. He must be all of a mile up. Around the pillar a great black spiral curved, its massiveness bound at intervals to the great pillar by smaller round members. He realized that he was on the outside, and that the spiral was the endless passage he had explored.

His body was seized with a violent shaking, and nausea filled his throat. A heavy chill descended on him as he lay, now too weak to move. He realized distantly that he must be going into shock. There was little hope, he thought foggily. He felt a vague sadness at the irony of ending his life in some unknown world a mile from sympathetic eyes far below.

Through fading sight, he saw the three beings drift out on the platform. The small Oriental was with them, his face now impassive, unconcerned. There were two other lean, manlike figures with him, and they came forward.

As consciousness faded, van der Reis was aware of hands touching him, of oddly articulated limbs grasping his body and lifting him up. Soft fabric covered him, sealing in his fading warmth. Through blackness, he felt himself change orientation. Dizzily he wondered if he were falling through space, if he would fall that great distance to die at the foot of the great obsidian pillar. His mathematician mind began with idiot precision to calculate how long it would take.

As the figures formed in his mind, a part of his departing consciousness thought quite critically: But you're assuming that you know the acceleration of gravity in this place. It may well not be the Earth.

He heard someone saying, "Norm, Norm." He opened his eyes and saw McDow's shadowed form by the door. He checked his watch quickly and said, "Why didn't you call me earlier?"

"You needed the sleep," McDow said.

Bayerd pushed to an upright position. "Thanks, Terry," he said tiredly. "This thing has begun to get to me. I'll admit that."

"You wouldn't be human if it didn't," McDow said with an odd twist to his face.

"Do I strike you as that inhuman sometimes?" Bayerd asked, noting the expression.

"No, no, nothing like that," McDow protested. "You alarm me the way you drive yourself. Sure, you're demanding of the other men, but I've seen how much you demand of yourself, just as though you were . . ."

"As though I were a whole man?" Bayerd accused.

"I didn't mean that."

"Well, hell, Terry," he said. "We both know what the situation is. You can't live inside a body that's turning to jelly on you and not admit you resent it. Perhaps that's why I still try to act as if I were stalking around under one 'g' and not feeling as limp as a kitten."

"We've heard from the *Orion*," McDow said. "The *CX-248* is a complete loss, but they rescued the balloon and put a spin on it. It unfolded in good shape."

"Have they started the charge buildup?"

"They're still building," McDow said. "They're 20

percent above the statcoulomb value we calculated as necessary for full deflection. If our path calculation is reasonably accurate, this should do it."

"How much time?"

"Ten minutes," McDow said.

"We'd better get topside," Bayerd said, swinging into his chair.

As they moved along the corridor to the levitator, McDow said, "The *Orion* has a nanosecond strobe unit. We should get some very good readings on beam azimuth if the beam falls within the field."

"Is there likely to be a problem with that?" Bayerd asked.

"They're fitting the unit with a wide-angle lens," McDow said. "I think we'll get the reading we want."

They found Mendoza on the bridge, watching the monitor. A moment after they entered, Adrianne appeared from the other hatch. Bayerd watched her move across the bridge with that fluid grace he had always so much admired. He was rather surprised when she said nothing, but positioned herself beside Mendoza. As he found a spot from which he could watch, he was disconcerted to see that she occasionally stole a glance at him. Her face reflected great puzzlement and . . . was it . . . worry, distaste? He couldn't analyze the expression.

"Thirty seconds," McDow said.

"Now we can only pray," Mendoza said.

McDow began to speak into the microphone before him as a dim image from the *Orion* built up on the screen. It was apparent that the *Orion* was part of the group of ships building up the charge on the inflated lens, for only the sterns of two of the ships showed in the screen at close range. The huge curve of the proplene sphere covered half of the screen, its metallic-plated sides gleaming in crescent. They had expanded the sphere by centrifugal force and then cut a hole in its side to position the cable. The sphere once expanded, of course, had maintained its shape.

"Five seconds!" McDow said.

Bayerd realized that he was not breathing and forced himself to inhale. *Pray God this will end it*, he thought.

"Zero," McDow said with a sigh.

"Get their readings," Bayerd commanded. The overhead speaker crackled suddenly as McDow cut it in for them to hear.

"B. F. Station," a voice said, "this is the *Orion*."

"B. F. Station to *Orion*. Did you get a reading?"

"We got one all right."

"How much deflection?"

"We couldn't measure it."

"What do you mean? What's the accuracy of your sighting?"

"You don't understand me," the voice said. "We clocked the beam right on schedule. The only problem is that it passed five miles outside of the volume you calculated for it."

Bayerd moved forward in front of McDow and snapped, "What's that again?"

The station intercom on the far side of the console was buzzing insistently. "Adrianne, get that thing," Bayerd said.

"You were way off, mister," the *Orion* voice said.

"This is Commander Bayerd. Explain yourself."

"Yes, sir," the man said.

"Norm," Adrianne's insistent voice cut through.

"Keep still," Bayerd snapped.

"It's Gilchrist," she insisted. "He's on 'S' level . . . down by the Shrenk cubicles."

"I said," the *Orion*'s man repeated, "you were way off. We didn't jog that beam one whisker."

"Gilchrist says Chang's team has collapsed the capsule tube. The capsule is buried under a ton of rock."

"What difference does it make now?" Bayerd said, sinking to a chair.

"You don't understand. Gilchrist has barricaded himself on 'S' level. He's warning us not to come down."

"What's got into him?" Mendoza demanded.

"He's given the men orders to blow up the accelerator," Adrianne said.

Chapter Eleven

H PLUS EIGHTEEN HOURS, THIRTY MINUTES

The (call it) time displacement area has extended over almost one-half of the globe now. In San Francisco Madame Clarrismo, medium of many and devious talents, is astonished at the success of her latest seance, and in the late afternoon in her somber chamber, shudders at the apparitions that have appeared and gone. On the Aleutian Islands of Attu and Kiska, natives are startled as bands of World War II Japanese soldiers appear, marching dispiritedly up the craggy beaches from ancient landing craft. In Los Angeles, a phantom earthquake shatters illusionary mains, and drenches the downtown area with a strange water that does not wet. The beaches along Baja California pound to the hoofbeats of *banditos* that vanished half a century before. A little later perhaps a ragtag band of rusty-armored Spaniards will stand on a peak in Panama and look out over the great ocean with a wild surmise. Now, lights burn in a strangely unweathered Mesa Verde, and paleolithic creatures crawl through the Louisiana Bayou country, rending the air with their hunting cries.

The news of the failure to predict the beam path spread through the Pelambang complex almost as soon as the event. They had, of course, been monitoring the transmissions, waiting for direct data from the *Orion*, and the captain's transmission to Bayerd had generated a wave of distress and depression that surged through the station like a flood tide. In minutes the crowds gathered outside knew of it, such was the efficiency of the grapevine by that time. Means called frantically for new troops as the crowds muttered ominously. Finally, knowing that this might help quiet the potential mob, he released the information that the accelerator was about to be destroyed. For some reason this satisfied the crowd, although several of the brighter members realized that this would in no way affect the destiny of the plasmoid stream, now about one and a half hours from the Earth-moon system.

For Carmelita and Martin the news was particularly depressing. Neither had slept for nearly eighteen hours, and now to see all of their work on the new banks utterly useless was the ultimate frustration. They were in Carmelita's small suite on the third level. She was brewing coffee and trying to maintain a tight hold on her nerves. Martin sat on the couch, equally silent.

He had been staring into the distance, absently watching the spiral of smoke from his cigarette. Suddenly, he snapped, "Damn."

She laughed bitterly. "That's a mild comment," she said.

"No," he said, "I mean about the model."

"How can you worry about that infernal model when we're faced with the present problem?"

"An idiot fixation," he said. "I suppose that's the thing that keeps me from panicking like those poor animals outside. There's an illusive unity in all of these phenomena. It has to be the tachyon flux. We assumed that, and it must be so."

"Here, I put sugar in it," she said, handing him a Thermos mug of coffee. She sat beside him, nursing her cup and idly rubbing her hand on the back of his neck. He leaned back and sighed at the animal pleasure of the massage. Funny, he thought, how they had battled for so long and in twenty hours had become so close.

"It's the problem of the time phenomena," he said tiredly. "I can't fit it into any existing models of the continuum. We know that in any tachyon interaction, the sequence of events will depend on the observer. They theorized this years ago when the tachyon was postulated. To one observer an atom will appear to emit a tachyon with recoil while to another observer, the same event will appear to be atom adsorbing a tachyon while moving to intercept it. The only acceptable hypothesis in such events is that all world lines exist to some observer displaced outside the real universe."

"That reality doesn't make too much sense," she said.

"No, I suppose not, but imagine that hypothetical observer. The initial and final entropic states of our universe are equally visible to him."

"But that implies that all world lines are fixed. How can time past or time future influence the present?"

"That, my girl," he said tiredly, "is the impossible question. Answer it for me and I'll love you forever."

She sat, wrapped in thought. "Oh, come on," he said. "You don't have to get involved in it."

"I wasn't," she said. "I could care less about your tachyon cosmos. I was more interested in another statement."

"Oh," he said and was surprised that he felt flushed. He lost himself in the contemplation of his cup. Finally he said, "It's true, you know."

"Yes," she said. "I know, but isn't it supposed to be that way in a metafamily?"

"Of course," he said. "We're very modern people, aren't we?"

"Are we?" she said. "I suppose you know that Gerta won't be with us very long. She and Means have found each other remarkably attractive, though why I can't say."

"Bitchy," he said laughing. Then, "Yes, I suppose so. Poor Karl, he has worked so hard to keep emotional stability in the unit. Now . . ."

"Now it's all dissolving," she said.

"All?" he asked, waiting tensely for an answer.

"All," she said with great finality.

He touched her lightly, wondering at the sudden excitement. "I had almost forgotten Karl," he said. "I've been terribly worried about him, but there's nothing we can do."

"Nothing whatsoever," she said, closing her eyes. He took her in his arms, feeling for the first time very guilty. He did the things he had done before when they cohabited and the rhythm built to the inevitable. He started to remove her tunic. Her hand stopped him.

"No, it's all different now," she said. "It's just you and me and it's all different."

"I suppose so," he said. Then he laughed. "My, but we're a worthy couple to inhabit my tachyon universe. Throwbacks to the Victorian period."

"Don't laugh," she said. "It really isn't funny. I want you, but it wouldn't be right. Not until we have Karl back and all the old ties are severed."

"Poor Karl," he said sincerely. "Wherever he is, I wish him well."

"He's a survivor type," she said. "He'll always come out."

"I hope so," he said fervently.

"What happened?" Mendoza demanded. "I thought you had the beam path pinned down."

"We did," Bayerd said.

"Where did we make the mistake?" Patel asked softly.

"That doesn't matter. There must be some way of stopping the beam," Mendoza said.

"And stopping that idiot Gilchrist from wrecking the accelerator," Bayerd said. "I'm going down there and try to reason with him."

"Wait a minute," Adrianne said suddenly. "We must have had the path of the beam calculated fairly well or it would never have struck the *SAU-62*. The small distance she traveled was just enough to bring her into the path."

"That was apparent enough," Bayerd said. Then he slapped his fist into the palm of the other hand and said excitedly, "The explosion! We weren't expecting that."

"I don't see . . ." she began.

"Radiant energy. Lots of it."

"The light pressure!" she exclaimed.

"Of course. The radiant energy of the explosion overtook the beam in a fraction of a microsecond. The light pressure was enough to distort the beam course slightly."

"But not enough."

She seated herself at the desk and began to feed information into the programmer of the station computer, occasionally referring to the sheaf of flimsies with the Earthside computer data. After a few moments, she looked up and said,

"This might do it. If we try for a hundred-kilometer displacement of the beam above the Earth's atmosphere, we're probably safe. So . . ." she touched the last sheet of her calculations, "if we touch off a reaction at . . . say, the distance of the Black Field Station . . . a million miles from Terra, we need a deflection of about twenty seconds to each plasmoid segment of the beam."

She continued to write rapidly and finally leaned back. "Under those conditions," she said, "it figures out to a hundred and twenty kilos of U-235 at 20 percent conversion."

Bayerd turned to face McDow. "Call Luna Station and get a ship, any ship loaded with enough fissionables. They can load a Black Field and set it up on the way out. Better make it two hundred kilos just to be safe."

"Can you do it in an hour and a half?" Mendoza asked.

"We can try," Adrianne said. "We must try."

"Just pray Luna can give us what we want," Bayerd said. "Now I've got to stop that idiot Gilchrist.

"I'm coming with you," Mendoza said.

They emerged from the personnel tube into the corridor leading toward the Shrenk cubicles. The pressure hatch sealing the compartment from the rest of the station was closed, blocking their view of the passage.

They were within twenty feet of the hatch when the intercom crackled and they heard Gilchrist say, "Bayerd, I know you're out there."

"Come on out," Bayerd said. "We've got to talk about this."

"We've talked enough," Gilchrist said. He sounded calm, with no trace of hysteria. "We've talked and talked for years and we have never agreed."

"You've got to call off the men," Bayerd said. "If you destroy the accelerator, we'll never be able to rebuild it."

"Don't you think I know that?" Gilchrist said. "But the consequences of destroying the Artery are a hell of a lot more attractive than the consequences of that transmission starting again."

"Wait," Mendoza said, "what about the lens stations?"

"Lens stations?" Bayerd said.

"Yes, the orbital magnetic lens that warps the beam above Pluto?"

"No chance," Bayerd said. "They're self-powered and keyed by c-cube radio to the control capsule. We can't change its position and we can't get a Shrenk body near one to turn off the field. Same problem as with the accelerator. The magnetic fields are too dense."

"There's another way," Mendoza said. "You can replace a lens station a lot easier than the Artery."

"Ram one with a ship?"

"Of course. Then the beam will head into space. It doesn't make any difference if every bit of the reserve metal within the accelerator area goes out. It won't strike anything."

"All right," Bayerd said. "Gilchrist, I'll make a deal with you. Let us through to Chang and I'll take one of the lens stations out of action. We can't let them touch the accelerator."

For long moments there was silence. Finally, the hatch door moved aside and Gilchrist stepped out. "You'll have to get out there immediately," he said. "They've already fueled one of the old supply ships. They're going to ram the accelerator with it."

"This was your ultimate solution, I suppose," Bayerd said bitterly. "The one thing that would justify your career."

"Don't be a fool," Gilchrist said. "Do you believe that I would want to destroy the Artery if there were any other way? It exists. It's a *fait accompli* that has cost billions and the lives of at least twelve people during its construction. Only a madman would destroy such an effort for his own ego." He stared at Bayerd contemptuously, "Or build it initially simply for his own ego," he added.

Bayerd gestured at his body. "If I had the strength in this body, I'd ram your words down your throat."

"There are other answers than violence," Gilchrist said. "You're a brilliant man, Bayerd. Why not use the strengths nature gave you instead of looking for some childish satisfaction?"

Bayerd turned to McDow and said, "Terry, I've got to get to the Shrenk cubicle before they do anything foolish out there."

McDow nodded silently. "It's the only way," he said. "We'll find an answer to it all. Only now we have to solve that part of the problem, and the destruction of one of the lens stations is the best answer."

Minutes later Bayerd was in the Shrenk harness and on Pluto. He had thought of pulling Chang from the neighboring cubicle, but he realized this would not stop the Earth-based men from their project of destruction. He made his way across the plain at a low run toward the field where the ships were berthed. He could see the men gathered around one of the ships as he approached. They were finishing the fueling, he saw. Two of the men whirled to face him as he came abreast of them.

"It's Bayerd," he said.

"Don't try to stop us, Commander," Trubner said. "This is the only solution left to us."

"I'm not trying to stop you," he said. "I'm just offering another target."

He explained the plan and Sanchez said, "All right, we'll try it. Chang was taking the ship out."

"That's right," Chang said.

"I'll take over that end," Bayerd said.

"No," Chang said, "I would rather . . ."

"That's an order," Bayerd said. "This is something that I have to do. I won't have anyone else touching the Artery."

"Of course," Chang said softly.

Van der Reis opened his eyes. He was lying comfortably on a small couch, his lower torso covered with a gauzelike coverlet that exuded a comforting warmth. He lay, luxuriating in the sheer animal feel of comfort. The lights of the room were subdued and the walls molded themselves about his couch in pleasant pastel contours that gave the illusion of a much larger room. It was, he realized, scarcely more than three meters by four, but he felt no sense of claustrophobia.

He sat up abruptly as memory returned. All those last moments of looking down the mile-high shaft of the strange building, the overwhelming shock enveloping his mind, the sight of his belly torn open by the claws of the great beast. He threw the coverlet from his body and realized that he was nude. Quickly he explored his lower abdomen. There was no sign of the terrible wound, not even a scar. His prodding fingers found a slight tenderness in the abdomen but nothing more.

While he was exploring this wonder, the wall before him flowed like putty and a perforation appeared. This grew larger in a second, and through the opening stepped a man. Van der Reis gasped automatically. The man looked for all the world like a younger version of Norman Bayerd, although his hair was a deep blue-black, whereas Bayerd's was brown.

He was wearing simple sandals, a pair of low-cut iridescent trunks, and nothing else. His upper torso was bare, and an intricate spiral design had been painted around each nipple in three shades of blue. He was full-chested and well-developed, as though he had spent a great deal of time in carefully designed athletics.

"I see you're feeling better," the man said briskly. "We decided to give you twenty-four hours. The wound itself, of course, was an easy thing to handle, but the nervous system does need time to recover. The purely emotional drain of shock, you know."

"Twenty-four hours?" van der Reis said. "Is that how long . . ."

"Well, actually about twenty-two," the man said. "The wound healed well in about five. Does that surprise you?"

"That sort of thing is completely beyond our technology," van der Reis said.

"Of course," the man said, smiling somewhat smugly. "However, we don't have too much time before we take you back to the resonator, and I need to give you a great deal of information."

"Is that what you call that thing, the structure I found myself in? A resonator?"

"A tachyon resonator," the man said. "We can't generate a major flux ourselves . . . rather we don't dare, but we built the resonator to use the flux you've been generating five centuries ago."

Van der Reis put his feet over the edge of the couch and looked about the room.

"I think we'd better be on our way," the man said.

"Where are my clothes?" van der Reis said.

"You won't need them," the man said. "It's quite

warm." Then he laughed. "Oh, of course, I suppose you still have a nudity taboo." He plunged his hand seemingly into the solid surface of the wall and withdrew a tunic and sandals. "I'm afaid your own clothing was in pretty bad shape after your encounter with the cave bear."

Van der Reis donned the tunic, which had a small belt attached, and stood up. "My name is Christopher Beard, by the way," the man said. "We've met before, I think."

"You remind me of someone I know," van der Reis said.

"Bayerd?" Beard said. "A distant relative. The name has changed a bit in the centuries, but I do look a bit like him."

"He has no children," van der Reis said.

Beard frowned. "He did have one," he said. "He would have to, you know. He's a very foolish and very brave man in many ways."

Beard gestured toward the open sphincter in the wall, and van der Reis followed him through it into a corridor with the same subdued lighting. "You sound as if you've met him," van der Reis said.

"In much the same way I have you," Beard said, moving at a good pace along the corridor. "We've tried various ways to get back to head off the disaster that is upon us. I saw you briefly in Pelambang, but I wasn't able to hold the contact."

"Oh," van der Reis said, remembering the unsettling moment when the dark man had addressed him as "priest." "I should have recognized you," he said.

"We can manipulate the past in person to a certain extent during this period when the tachyon flux is high. The only sure way, however, was to bring you forward. It seems we gathered a few unwanted fish in our net."

Van der Reis rubbed the place where the wound had healed and thought that they had gathered some rather deadly fish.

They entered a large chamber through another of the sphincter doors, and van der Reis was surprised to see the small Oriental standing against the far wall. The man's eyes widened as he recognized van der Reis, and he bowed deeply. Ranged against the far wall were several upholstered contour chairs, now occupied by two men, one apparently in his late teens, the other older and more solid-looking and of an undefinable age.

The older man rose. Van der Reis was surprised to see that he was nearly seven feet tall, with a massive musculature and broad, flat fingers covered with a coarse growth of reddish hair.

"We don't have too much time," the man said. "Joakim and I have decided that we have about four hours before we must return you and our unfortunate friend, Mr. Fusaka, to your own time." At the mention of his name the small Oriental smiled nervously.

"Joakim is rather your counterpart in this era," Beard said. "I'm sure you can find a common language."

The young man smiled and said, "I think we can give you all of the information you need in an hour." He spoke with a deep, resonant voice, almost singing the words. Swedish, van der Reis thought.

"I'm Okada," the big man said. "I can't fill you in with the complete details of our project, but I hope to impress you with the absolute necessity of what we must do."

"Which is?" van der Reis said.

"The Artery must be destroyed," Okada said fiercely. He said it with the same intensity a Roman might have said, *Carthago delenda est.*

"Impossible," van der Reis said. "The Earth would sink to barbarism without the Artery."

"Yet, it has not," Joakim said, spreading his hands. "Here is the evidence that it has not."

"You mean that the Artery was destroyed in your past?" van der Reis said. "Then why go to such fantastic lengths to bring me here and convince me that this must be?"

"History is a snare for us all," Beard said. "We do this because our history said we did. This is not to say that world lines are fixed and immutable. Ordinarily they are, but your Artery and specifically your Black Field have created a situation in which all things can change."

"More than this," Joakim said, "we face a very real possibility that the continued existence of the Artery in your time can destroy . . . I don't quite know how to put it." He spread his hands, shaping an imaginary sphere. "It can destroy existence . . . reality, the meta-universe itself."

"This means nothing to me," van der Reis said. "I don't know what you're saying."

"Of course you don't," Okada said fiercely. "That's why we must show you. Joakim, this is your job."

The boy rose to his feet. "I can't give you the background on all this. You've been attempting to develop a model to explain the phenomena associated with the tachyon flux, but you've been too conservative. Besides, your geometry is incapable of handling an infinite-order Lobachvskian projection."

"There are too many contradictions," van der Reis said. He'd toyed with the idea at odd moments. A geometry derived from the unprovable Euclidean postulate that through a point one and only one line could be drawn parallel to a given line. If one assumed no parallel lines, one derived spherical geometry in which all lines on the surface were great circles and inevitably intersected. Postulate two possible parallel lines, and one derived the geometry for something called a pseudosphere, which looked very much like two trumpets laid bell to bell with their stems extending without limit. On this surface the two lines approached the third asympototically but never met it. To imagine geometry in which any number of lines without limit could be drawn through a single point parallel to a given line . . . it created a maze of contradictions. The idea of imagining such a surface to which one could apply such a geometry . . . it was completely beyond the limitations of a human mind.

The thought startled him. He looked at Joakim, and suddenly he knew with a blend of awe and horror that such a concept was indeed beyond human ability. The boy was ageless, he realized, and very unhuman. The intuition must have shown in his expression. Joakim smiled distantly and said, "But, you see, this was the reason I was brought into being."

Beard took van der Reis back to the resonator chamber along a high walkway above the city. Van der Reis at first felt uneasy, suspended so high in space with only the unsubstantial walkway beneath him. There was no apparent support of the long, sweeping path other than its own substance. Beard smiled at him and said, "It's quite safe."

In the central section of the resonator building, Beard paused and said, "You must convince the others of the importance of what you've learned. Bayerd, of course, is of no importance."

"I don't think you fully understand Bayerd's nature," van der Reis objected.

"After meeting Joakim, you can say such a thing?" Beard laughed. "I probably know more about your special bank than anyone in your time, perhaps even more than you do. You may recall that I spent some time examining it on the several occasions I was able to get back."

"You could have done a great deal of damage," van der Reis said.

Beard frowned. "I've done what I had to do. Had we not been able to transmit this information, we would have at least halted the process that now threatens to overwhelm us."

He left van der Reis in the resonator hub. As he had been instructed, van der Reis made his way along the spoke to the outer spiral. There he lowered himself to the curved floor, his back against one wall, and waited. The operation of the resonator was highly unpredictable, Beard had told him, depending on the flux surge near the Black Field Station. They had developed a complex statistical treatment of the effect so that he could be assured of a surge in the resonator within the next hour. (The nanosecond-long surges in his own time were attenuated over the centuries and manifested themselves as surges separated by from thirty minutes to two hours.)

He wondered what must be happening in his own time. The Artery emergency had been so far from his mind that this was the first time he had found a chance to return to his original concern. He thought of Martin and Carmelita with a small glow of pleasure. It would be so good to see them again, if only he could arrive in time.

Time, he thought ironically. He had all the time in the universe, all the time in an infinate number of universes.

He remembered the projection that appeared in the middle of the room as he and Joakim had talked. The hologram had entranced him, even though Joakim assured him that the representation was a crude analogy only, that it was impossible to illustrate the complexity of the meta-universe in a simple three-dimensional model.

"The basic postulate," Joakim said, "is that all world lines are fixed in space and time to some observer removed from our universe."

"But that means that one would have to view time as another spatial dimension," van der Reis objected.

"Of course," Joakim said with a faint smile. "One might represent our universe . . . say . . . as a cylinder or actually as a closed toroid." He gestured with his hand, and the model cylinder formed in the hologram. "The figure is composed of layers without end, each representing a discrete entropy state, a time state, if you will, since time has no meaning unless we consider time 'A' in the two states. The total layers or entropy states then represent our universe progressing from minimum to maximum entropy, the whole array of world lines."

"Well, that's easy enough if you accept the real existence of each state in some universe," van der Reis said, "But the tachyon phenomenon . . ."

"At a point of high-tachyon flux, we develop a statistical anomaly," Joakim said patiently. "The canonical assembly we might write to describe a closed system of entropy cells in the 'now' ceases to have meaning. In this spatial area, where the tachyon flux is maximum, entropy may assume all values between the maximum and the minimum simultaneously. It were as if you had compressed at one point all of the infinite layers within our three-dimensional model so that all were in contact. In this area the cross section of entropy surfaces would have a zero dimension."

Van der Reis watched the holographic cylinder invaginate from the top and bottom so that the representative layers that Joakim had pointed out in the model streched from both the top and bottom and came into contact at one spot within the cylinder. The spot, of course, represented his own time, where tachyon flux was being generated. "Within the area," van der Reis said slowly, "all world lines are in contact from the beginning of the universe to the end."

"Roughly yes," Joakim said. "Although I ask you to remember that a toroid would be a better three-dimensional model than the cylinder that we are using. Our own space-time continuum obviously does not have such dimensional boundaries. There are other universes like ours in the meta-universe, of course, numberless other universes that have point-for-point congruencies with ours in n-space."

Van der Reis's head swam with the concept. It was completely impossible to visualize it except in the crudest analogy. "The problem," Joakim said laconically, "is that at this point of tachyon flux, which is a characteristic of the Black Field, we establish similar interactions with other universes in n-space, and some of these universes, actually exactly half of them, have entropy flows exactly opposite ours."

"But that means that if we establish full congruency, one could heterodyne the other, cancel it out."

"Which is exactly what is about to happen," Joakim said, "unless we end the Black Field operation. Haven't you ever wondered where all of the partition energy is going? Energy is completely disappearing within the Black Field, and it has to go somewhere."

"Of course," van der Reis said. "We're not fools. We've speculated for many years on this."

"Under ordinary circumstances, every geodesic in metaspace is parallel to every other, even though this implies parallel lines without limit through a given metaspace point. Your careless dissipation of energy through the Black Field is altering this. For our universe in the Earth-moon area, that parallelism is breaking down."

Van der Reis shook his head. Then he realized that there were implications to this that even Joakim hadn't considered. The sudden excitement that appeared on his face caused the mathematician to smile. "I see," Joakim said, "that you have seen the obvious answer to your immediate crisis and to your long-term power crisis."

"It could well mean the end of one world and the beginning of another," he said.

"For my world, unless that world changes because of what you are doing in yours, that is exactly what happened," Joakim said.

Van der Reis stretched his legs out on the obsidian floor and contemplated the disaster that was almost upon them. It would not be dramatic. If the phantom universe of which they spoke and his own achieved full congruency, both would simply cease to exist. There would be nothing dramatic about it. To that hypothetical observer beyond n-space the two universes would never have existed. Undoubtly there were other Earths and perhaps even other van der Reises, but for him, for this consciousness, there would be no existence, and indeed there would never have been an existence. He shuddered at the thought.

The Artery had to be destroyed, no doubt of that. The power needs of the world, however, would not go unfilled. For they had poured energies into this other universe that could now be trapped and more, could be trapped anywhere in his real (?) universe. If only he could get back in time.

He laughed abruptly at his use of the word. Time had no meaning, not really. He would or he would not find himself back in the spot on that hypothetical entropy surface that represented his time. If he did, then there was no problem. It was all in the hands of some unknown statistical god who had put the whole complex mess together at some unimagined time in the past or in the future. From that, he could . . .

The transition was instantaneous. There was no warning, just a sudden change in lighting, a momentary disorientation as his position changed in space and . . .

He was in Pelambang. In the spot within the computer array that he had always so carefully guarded from the eyes of others. Only he was not wearing an optical suit. He heard the first sounds from the alarm.

My God, he thought. Norm, what have I done, and he pushed to his feet, throwing himself across the small programming cubicle to the override panel. He wasn't sure he had made it before the damage was done.

Pluto was a fast-receding speck of light in the ship's viewplate. Bayerd was crowding the ship to the limit of its nine gravities acceleration, but the Shrenk body gave no sensation of weight. Hurriedly he checked the time. An hour and ten minutes left.

He switched the viewplate to the forward pickup and saw at a distance the points of light that were the lens stations, revolving ceaselessly around a common center. Carefully he corrected his course and locked the controls. Then he waited, checking the collision course at intervals. He knew when the magnetic field from the stations began to build up. The legs of the robot became imbued with a life of their own. They quivered, and one lashed out against the bulkhead. He was losing his balance, falling . . . and in the next instant all sight and sound faded and he was an ordinary flesh-and-blood man, embraced in a tight womb of blackness. He waited for long moments for control to return. All at once he was again in the Shrenk body.

He was wallowing in space, his metal body turning slowly like some dancer in a dream ballet. Around him the debris of the ship moved in complex patterns, colliding and bouncing away, still sharing his velocity and path. He thrashed his arms about, trying to stabilize his motion. In one slow turn he saw the lens.

The station he had destroyed was flaring brightly as its power piles erupted. It was falling into the center of the lens, he saw, and in the next turn he saw that the other stations were moving.

In the instant before he cut control of the body, he realized what he had done. The lens stations were falling in on each other, destroying each other as the equilibrium of their system was destroyed.

He was sick with the sight as he pulled from the restraining harness. Mendoza was waiting outside the cubicle, and he pushed past him without speaking.

On the Commo Bridge he lowered his body until his head was between his legs, trying to fight off the sudden wave of dizziness.

"Norm," Beckworth said, "are you all right?"

"I'll be fine in a minute," he said.

"We're finished anyway," McDow said quietly.

"Leave him alone for a minute," Beckworth said.

"What do you mean, we're finished?" Bayerd demanded, raising his head.

"He means there's not a ship within flight distance," Mendoza said.

"It was a pretty idea," McDow said, "but we'll never get to see if it works."

Bayerd shook his head, feeling a sudden roar in his ears.

"Unless . . ." he heard Adrianne say.

"Unless what?" McDow said.

"If we can reverse the polarity of the Black Field."

"Here? This station?"

"It's the only solution left."

Bayerd pushed Beckworth away and turned to face her.

"That's what you've wanted all along," he said, fiercely. "You've rigged this whole thing to destroy the Artery."

"What are you saying?" Adrianne demanded, her voice pained and trembling.

"Norm, you'd better stop now," Beckworth said, placing a restraining hand on Bayerd's shoulder. "You're fatigued and too overwrought to know what you are saying."

"Keep away from me," he said hoarsely. "Of course I'm tired. Who wouldn't be? But that doesn't mean I've lost my sense of proportion. The Artery has been deliberately sabotaged, and the pattern is quite clear."

"Stop it," McDow said. "You don't know what you're saying."

"Norm, there's so much you don't understand," Adrianne said.

"I understand enough," he said angrily. "I have all of the evidence I need. It was Adrianne who changed the capsule settings. Had she understood better what she was doing, this might not have happened, but it was she."

"That's a terrible accusation," Mendoza said.

"The monitoring tapes would have proved it," Bayerd said. "You know what happened to me in the cubicle when I was checking them out. Who was it who attacked me? You or Gilchrist. He has to be in it with you."

"Attack?" she said. "What kind of madness are you talking about?"

"Someone hit me, stole the tapes."

"No one attacked you," McDow said tiredly. "What happened to you has a more rational explanation than that."

Adrianne shook her head sadly. "So, at last the truth must come out. How long do you think you could have carried on this impossible pretense?"

"How could you know?" McDow began.

"It's sufficient that I know. It is perhaps better now that Norm know as well."

"What are you talking about?" Bayerd demanded.

"No one attacked you," McDow said sadly. "There wasn't any incriminating tape in Adrianne's cubicle."

"I suppose that I imagined it all. Tell me all about fatigue and the need to fabricate such a fantasy."

"It is something that we must now consider," Beckworth said slowly.

Bayerd scarcely heard him in the sudden unreasoning hatred that seemed to possess his body. The feeling washed over him.

"You've tried to destroy the Artery and me ever since we first met," he shouted. "Now your little underhanded trick has turned on you." He pulled the coded message flimsy from his pocket. "The whole pattern gets pretty clear, this message to one of your plants on my crew, your sabotaging the capsule . . ."

She rose slowly and took the flimsy from Bayerd's hand, glanced at it, and looked up.

"This isn't mine," she said. "You, of all people, should know who this one was sent to."

"And you know there's no evidence on that monitoring tape from Adrianne's cubicle," McDow said. "It's the original tape. She couldn't have faked it in that detail."

Bayerd felt the blood roaring in his ears. The room was suddenly dark, with shadows crouching in every corner.

"This is the administrative code the computer sections use," Adrianne was saying. "Only top brass has the code, and you're the only top brass here."

"No," Bayerd said. "It's all a part of the plot. Destroy the Artery. Discredit me."

"I didn't stop with Adrianne's tape, " McDow said. "I checked the one from your cubicle. You were still in control of the robot at the capsule site up until the moment the crew arrived to seat the capsule."

The room was awash with blackness. A horrible quivering had seized the muscles of Bayerd's thighs.

"And there was nothing wrong with the calibration of your instruments on the console at the Needle," McDow was saying.

"Damn it, cut it out," Beckworth yelled.

"It was Bayerd," McDow said. "He was the one who received the code message. He was the one who changed the vernier settings on the capsule at the last moment."

Something was terribly wrong. All support seemed to disappear from his body. He was falling down a deep black tube. Nausea washed over him, and for a second it seemed as if his very ego were dissolving, shattering.

"My God, what's wrong with him?" he heard Mendoza's voice.

"Not him," McDow said. "Pelambang. Something terrible has happened at Pelambang."

Fingers were prying open his eyes while something cold and metallic touched the base of his third cervical vertebra. Dimly through a roaring that seemed to bury his brain in blackness, he heard Beckworth say,

"Terry, get Pelambang quickly. Tell him to activate the override. There's some sort of feedback. It'll destroy him."

"My God," he heard Adrianne say before blackness overwhelmed him, "what kind of men are you that you wouldn't let him die in peace?"

Chapter Twelve

H PLUS NINETEEN HOURS, FIFTEEN MINUTES

He could hear them talking from a great distance. At first he could not identify one voice, but finally he realized with some surprise that it was van der Reis's. Van der Reis? Back? What could have happened to the man?

Van der Reis was saying, "I've restored power to the unit. He should regain consciousness soon."

"What a terrible thing," Adrianne Patel said. "I knew that he had been badly injured in the accident, but I had no idea that . . ."

"That the being we know as Norman Bayerd had ceased to exist?" McDow said tiredly. "What would you have had us do? We needed him, not only as a symbol of the project but we needed his unique knowledge, his special driving ability."

"It was my fault, I suppose," van der Reis said. "Or my credit, depending on how you look at it. We had done this sort of thing before. The scanning techniques were well developed. With the peculiarly autocratic control I had here at Pelambang, it was easy enough to isolate one whole section, to re-create the personality, all of the intricate neuronic interchanges that make up a man."

Beckworth said, "The transceiver, itself, that replaced the frontal lobes was another matter. We spent a lot of time before we established myoelectric linkages that would be reliable."

"But what have you built, a mere robot," Adrianne protested.

"Not at all," McDow said. "The man you knew and the man you know now are identical, not the same, but certainly identical."

"But more vulnerable," van der Reis said. "It was Beard who found that peculiar vulnerability. He had to destroy the Artery in whatever fashion available to him. He managed to get to the computer complex several times and override the ego function, to use Bayerd even though he did not know he was being used."

"He did know," van der Reis said. "He must have suspected for some time, subconsciously. Maybe that isn't the word I want, but a part of him knew. That's why he sent the program through, the one that the message was about. A part of him couldn't accept the results, but he knew. Otherwise, his programming would have overridden Beard's attempt. He wanted the Artery destroyed as much as Beard did."

"I can't believe that," she said.

"He's been working through the same problem. He has all of the information now, what he surmised and what Beard and his colleagues have given me."

"It's the only explanation," she said. "The Artery was his whole life. Now I have to end even that." He heard her move away and heard the door behind her.

Yes, he thought, wading through darkness, *my whole life*. There was nothing that could force him to damage the Artery. It was the single thing he must leave behind after . . .

And then the memory came back.

The weeks of work over the new idea, the sudden realization that what he had found spelled the death of the Artery. How had he forgotten . . . the feeling of loss when he realized that it had all been for nothing . . . the sacrifice, the work . . . that the Artery was a useless toy, a vast, clumsy, makeshift answer when the simpler solution had been before them all the time. . . .

Who wouldn't have fled from the knowledge that his life had been useless?

Only . . . only there was always a part of a man that demanded that he act in truth and honesty . . . and if he did not, that inner self would find a way. . . .

And now, he saw with wonder, the knowledge was complete. All of the bits together. The knowledge of his own badly damaged body should have told him. The loss of pituitary function might have come about as they said, but it was more probable that the damage had been more extensive. How extensive he now knew.

He opened his eyes and sat up. He was in the dispensary, he saw, and McDow and Beckworth had withdrawn somewhat from his bed. They hadn't removed his clothing, he saw. Adrianne was nowhere to be seen. They were talking with a Shrenk robot and it was from this, he realized, that van der Reis's voice had proceeded.

"How long have I been out?" he demanded.

"Fifteen minutes," Beckworth said, moving toward him. "Now lie down until it's time."

"Time for what?"

"We're evacuating the station in another ten minutes or so. Adrianne is going to reverse the Black

Field. She has the engineering crew below making the modifications now."

Bayerd threw back the sheet they had draped over him. "Help me to my chair," he demanded.

"Get back in bed," Beckworth said.

"I've got to see her," he said.

"No, absolutely not. You can't stop her anyway."

"No," Bayerd said, "I don't want to stop her."

"You're in no condition . . ."

"Please, Doc. This is important."

Van der Reis's voice said, "Norman, my old dear friend, do you understand?"

"Of course," Bayerd said. "There's no need for sorrow. You did a great many things for me. I suppose the other life, my little secret body in New York was your doing?"

"It seems best," van der Reis said. "It was really the least I could do for you."

"Does she exist?" he asked. "Is she real?"

The robot body made an ineffectual gesture. "What is reality?" van der Reis said.

"Yes," Bayerd said, "That is something I, of all people, should never question. Not the nature of reality."

"Norm," McDow said, "we're moving to evacuate everyone in the station."

"Not everyone," Bayerd said. "Someone has to stay behind. You can't depend on a remote triggering."

"That," McDow said slowly, "is my job."

"No," Bayerd said. "I can handle it better than you and besides," he paused, considering the irony of the statement, "besides, I have a great deal less to lose than you."

"He's right, of course," Beckworth said.

"I have only a body to lose," Bayerd said, "and that hasn't been of much value for a long time."

"I am not sure that the psyche can survive an apparent death," van der Reis said slowly.

"You call this survival?" Bayerd said, gesturing at his body. "Now, help me into the chair and continue the evacuation."

McDow sighed resignedly and both he and Beckworth came forward, lifting his body gently from the bed and positioning it in the prosthetic chair.

"Where is she?" he saked.

"On the Commo Bridge," McDow said.

"All right," Bayerd said. "You have your instructions."

He maneuvered his chair through the irised door and into the corridor. As he made his way to the metering bridge, he felt a kind of nervous strength flowing into his muscles. He found her on the bridge in the midst of confusion.

Someone had unbolted several of the control panels on the bridge consoles, ripping wire from the back and inserting hasty cross connections. She looked up as Bayerd entered and said, "Norm, get below. There's not much time."

"How are you going to keep the five stations phased until the last moment?" Bayerd demanded.

"It'll be done."

"How?"

"Manually. How else?"

"I thought so. Now, listen closely. You were right about the code message. It was from the computer section at Pelambang. I had it coded for the simple reason that I didn't want anyone at the station to know what I working on."

"It makes no difference now," he said.

"Yes, it does," he said. "Van der Reis's data are the final confirmations. The whole problem has to do with the basic nature of the Black Field. The idea came to me, but I didn't have the full model I needed until now; but the idea is workable."

"I don't understand," she said.

"The solution was there all the time," Bayerd said. "We had the reverse field effect, releasing all that energy. We knew all about the microcontinuum the physicists had postulated and how the energy that came from the reversed field was the energy that had been poured earlier into the microcontinuum. Don't you see? The micro-universe had a point-for-point congruency with our universe, if we can believe van der Reis. You can put energy into it and later take that energy out . . . *and you don't have to perform the operation at the same point.*"

She was suddenly laughing, her small frame shaking with mirth. "It was there all along," she said. "We've never needed the Artery."

"No." Bayerd said. "We can generate the power right on Pluto, shunt it via the Black Field into the microcontinuum, after we've drained it, and draw on that power any place in the system."

"No," she said, "any place in the universe."

"Now," Bayerd said, "we've got the problem of the beam. Are you through up here?"

"Yes," she said. "The fields will have to be balanced manually on all of the stations in the Black Field up to the moment of reversal. I've wired the circuits into the controls in one of the Shrenk cubicles so we can use the c-cube transmitter on 'S' level."

"Thank you," he said. "We'll use my transmitter."

"You?" she said in surprise.

"Can you think of anyone more suited to the job?" he demanded. "McDow will go with you and the rest."

She nodded, her eyes showing her pain. "It seems like such a long time," she said. "So many years and so many harsh words and then suddenly we're working to the same goal again."

"With more sense," he said. Then, "There is one question I have to ask you."

"This man Beard of whom van der Reis spoke. He must have been the one I saw at one point. I remember how familiar he looked, and now I think I know why."

"I'm sorry," she said. "Perhaps it was selfish of me to conceal it, but we had grown so far apart and I was afraid of what you might have made of him."

"Well," he said, "it's enough to know that he exists. There's something very special to a man in having a son."

"He's a fine, a remarkable young man," she said. "Very much like his father."

"God, I hope not," Bayerd said wryly.

The intercom crackled and McDow's voice said, "We don't have too much time to get away. Adrianne, we're waiting for you in the shuttle."

She hesitated. "There's so much more I could say," she said.

"Most of it doesn't have to be said," Bayerd said.

She leaned over and kissed him lightly, not with passion as she once had done, but with a kind of blending of love and regret that very nearly made him lose control of himself.

"Goodbye," he said.

"Goodbye," she said and hurried to the hatch.

Bayerd turned to the console and finished the check that Adrianne had started. After a moment, a light glowed on a far panel and he knew that the shuttle had closed its airlock.

He flicked the switch that cut in the transmitter relay on the bridge and said, "This is Bayerd, calling the shuttle. You have fifteen minutes."

"I think that's enough," McDow said. The light flickered on the console, telling him that they had discharged from the shuttle hatch.

He began to make the final changes in the console, all the while speaking to them as the shuttle raced from the station.

"You'll be getting out of the system now, going to the stars, something we could never have dreamed of before." He laughed and said, "Name a planet after me." After that he cut the transmission.

At five minutes to calculated contact time with the beam, he abandoned the bridge and hurried down to the Shrenk cubicle, which Patel had modified. He laced himself into the harness and made the changes on the improvised board at its side, which initiated the change in polarity and the building instability of the Black Field. Then, as the bridge chronometer signaled two minutes to the board, he threw in the automatic system, keyed to the strobe units on the skin of the station.

"There," he said at fifty seconds before "zero," "the rest is up to you."

He pushed his head into the Shrenk facepiece. "Look on my works, ye Mighty, and despair!" he whispered, keying the unit.

For an instant he was in the body on far Pluto,

poised on the edge of the Needle, looking down the precipice into the chasm far below.

He would fall into the great fissure, he saw, fall like a stone into the far depths at the instant the Artery ceased to exist.

Which was as it should be. The final irony.

He thought of the Artery, its vainglory, and those ancient kings of Egypt whose time-dusted eyes had looked upon their magnificent tombs.

Then he quickly switched to the body beyond the Plutonian Magnetic Lens, still holding static control of the body on Pluto.

He was surrounded with the debris of the wrecked ship, but he was still moving at an incredible velocity. The last flare of energy from the colliding lens station must have accelerated him, he thought.

It was then that he realized that he was probably moving at a velocity greater than the escape velocity of the system.

That he was moving out to the stars.

While the Artery would signal his going in a blaze of light.

"A damned magnificent tomb," he thought.

And the cold Plutonian rock of the Needle with that one fraction of his consciousness, and the other part of him that was moving out to the stars . . . all this dissolved in fire as the thing that was his life spark expanded in a wave of radiance until it seemed to encompass the universe in searing light and ceased to be.

Epilogue

After he had spoken with Carmelita and Martin, van der Reis walked dejectedly down the corridor to the main programming room. The hustle had abated now that the danger of the Artery had passed, and technicians stood about, talking in quiet voices. He felt somehow completely alienated from them, as though his life had ended like the organic shell that had been called Norman Bayerd.

He was basically a conservative, he told himself, and he had tried to order his life in terms of a pattern that he thought made sense to his own ego. He had not counted on others deviating from that pattern.

No matter, he told himself resignedly. They were lovely people, those two, handsome and well made for each other. He felt a vague regret that he could no longer share in that special feeling that had grown between them. Perhaps it would last, perhaps not. He was enough of a cynic to tell himself that you took the good of the present, and when it ceased being what you wanted, you walked away and sought another good. He hoped that they could be as realistic.

For him there remained the work and the new unexplored avenues opened by his talk with Joakim. He would have a very real and important part in this new world they would soon be building. It was a world that Norman Bayerd should have lived in, but he had finally succeeded in contributing to the one dream he could never have realized before.

He stopped and, impelled by a need to know, he donned his optical suit and took the levitator to the forbidden level. At the silent panel, he paused and began to summon the tonal readouts. The array still functioned, and he supposed that therein the synthetic personality of Norman Bayerd still existed, as though in a dream. Funny that Beard, who had come across him that time, should have likened his present stance to that of a priest in the confessional booth.

His hands played over the induction plate. The response told him what he needed. Well, he had one final duty.

He made the changes that would assure the continuation of the residue of Bayerd in the pleasant world he had built for him somewhere in a dream New York. He would dream the dream forever, and if it were only one machine communicating with another, still it had a special kind of satisfaction to van der Reis.

He thought pleasantly of Martin and Carmelita and wished them well. Then he remembered back to that frightening world of the future where he had been briefly and had been nearly destroyed by a monster from the very other end of time. What had been the little Oriental's name? Fusaka? Well, he hoped he had made it back safely to whatever world of sanity he valued.

He sat and thought for a long time before he rose and went down again into the busy world of people and ideas and new worlds already about to be born.

Fusaka knew that somewhere they were watching

him. He stood silently in the obsidian chamber of the resonator and waited. Perhaps he would return, perhaps not. It was beyond hoping. His skin began to prickle, and he was surprised to see that its surface was emitting a faint blue brush discharge. Even as he watched, all sight faded, and in the next instant he was floating in complete darkness. He was tumbling then, not physically but rather as if the coordinates of space about him were rotating rapidly. Lights flickered, dazzling his eyes and then . . .

He was standing looking up at the morning sky. About him crowds of people hurried past. The women, black-haired and in cotton kimonos. One older woman, a child carried papooselike on her back, stumbled against him. Her eyes widened and she bowed, mumbling, "Gomen kudasai."

He exhaled vigorously. He was back, back to the world of sanity. Not back in Hokkaido as they had planned, but certainly back in his own land. A vintage car rumbled past, the charcoal burner in its trunk belching smoke. A clatter of voices assailed his ears and above that the distant keening of an air raid siren.

No one seemed particularly concerned about the siren. Several people stopped and pointed into the sky where the contrail of a single plane etched a billowing line across the cloud-speckled sky. He wondered at their unconcern and stopped a policeman who was hurrying past. The policeman shrugged. "It is nothing," he said. "Only a single aircraft. There have been many such false alarms in the past week."

"But it is a bomber," Fusaka said.

"Probably it has strayed from the pack," the policeman said and hurried on.

Near the edge of the city antiaircraft guns began a

a desultory barrage. Puffs of smoke appeared in front of the plane but it forged steadily ahead. It was nearly overhead now and, as he watched, something tumbled from its open bomb doors and tumbled for a distance before a parachute blossomed. Whatever it was that was descending, Fusaka saw that it was quite large, certainly larger that the clustered firebombs that had fallen on the cities before.

Someone near him gasped, and he looked up to see the wing of the plane suddenly disappear in a burst of smoke. The forward motion of the plane carried it past this point, and he saw that the wing was shredded, its debris trailing away in the slipstream. Seconds later the plane dipped and began to spiral down, heading for the edge of the city.

He watched the parachute drift forward. It was heading directly toward his area, and he felt a sudden alarm. Suppose it were a bomb. Certainly it was some kind of weapon. Why else drop it with such elaborate arrangements for parachuting it to safety? People were running about him now, their voices crying out in alarm. He knew that there was no point in running. If the thing were a bomb, it would be upon them in less than half a minute. The chute was ribboned so that the object was falling quite rapidly. He watched as a nearby building, its roof gone, hid the chute for a second and then he saw that it would fall in the square scarcely a block away.

He began to move toward the square, wondering why he did so. A curious feeling of need possessed him, and as he rounded the corner, he saw the thing strike the ground and the parachute flutter about it.

Nothing happened.

The device lay there, emitting some drifting smoke

but little else. He sniffed the air and realized that the smoke was some kind of pyrotechnic . . . cordite or some other smokeless powder, he decided. He circled the area cautiously as fire-fighting equipment charged into the square and a policeman . . . the same one, Fusaka saw . . . yelled at him.

From his vantage point he could see the blue-black device quite clearly. He remembered seeing something like it in those days before he had been wounded. Some of the captured equipment in the Philippines, he remembered. Except for some puzzling devices at one end, Fusaka thought, it looked for all the world like a shortened section of an American fifteen-inch naval gun barrel.

He puzzled this mystery as excited crowds surged forward about him. High in the bright morning sky a B-29 bomber that had once been christened the *Enola Gay*, its port wing shattered, plunged in a spiraling shriek for a group of shattered houses on the edge of Hiroshima. Later, Fusaka would determine that he had returned to his real world at about 8:00 A.M. on the morning of August 6, 1945.

It was a day that was otherwise unremarked in the bloody history of the war. Quite as unremarkable as August 9, three days later, when a somewhat similar morning incident was the source of great derision later that day in the newspages of the Nagasaki *Mainichi Shimbun.*

12-73

SEE OTHER SIDE ➧